Frank H. Hamilton

Fracture of the Patella

a study of one hundred and twenty-seven cases

Frank H. Hamilton

Fracture of the Patella
a study of one hundred and twenty-seven cases

ISBN/EAN: 9783337370749

Printed in Europe, USA, Canada, Australia, Japan

Cover: Foto ©Andreas Hilbeck / pixelio.de

More available books at **www.hansebooks.com**

A STUDY OF

One Hundred and Twenty-Seven Cases.

BY

FRANK H. HAMILTON, A.M., M.D., LL.D.,

Visiting Surgeon to Bellevue Hospital; Consulting Surgeon to
the Hospital for the Ruptured and Crippled, New York;
Author of "A Practical Treatise on Fractures and
Dislocations," "A Treatise on Military Surgery,"
"A Treatise on the Principles and Prac-
tice of Surgery," &c., &c., &c.

NEW YORK :
CHAS. L. BERMINGHAM & CO.,
MEDICAL PUBLISHERS,
1880.

PRINTED BY

W. L. MERSHON & CO.

RAHWAY, N. J.

FRACTURE OF THE PATELLA.

A Study of One Hundred and Twenty-Seven Cases.

No one, so far as I know, has attempted to record and carefully study any large number of cases of fracture of the patella. It has seemed to me, therefore, that it might be profitable to do so, inasmuch as my own personal experience and the records at Bellevue Hospital furnish probably not less than 130 cases, most of which have been faithfully recorded.

I shall publish first the cases which have come under my own observation, numbering 54 ; and subsequently those not seen by me, which have been admitted to Bellevue Hospital.

My final conclusions or inferences I shall reserve for a third paper; preferring at first to lay the cases before the reader, permitting him to study them for himself and make his own inferences. We shall then be able to consider the various points illustrated with a better mutual understanding.

There is no impropriety, however, in my calling the attention of the reader to some of the points which have already attracted my attention. He will note:—1. The large proportion of simple transverse fractures, and the infrequency of comminuted and compound fractures. 2. The frequency of fracture from muscular action. 3. The frequency of early joint effusions. 4. The difficulty which has constantly been experienced in securing and maintaining apposition of the fragments. 5. The great variety of methods which have been adopted, and the frequent changes made in the treatment of the individual cases ; either because of their inefficiency, or because of the pain and excoriations or other more serious injuries which they have occasioned ; and the equally good results where the attempts to get close union have been less assiduous. 6. The uniformity of a fibrous union, with some separation. 7. The frequency of a re-fracture, and its more serious results. 8. The frequency of anchylosis, and its proportion to the time the limb is kept in splints. 9. The great time which elapses before the functions of the limb are restored.   10. The inadequacy of the ordinary knee-caps while the patients walk about.   11. The remarkable power of restoration of the functions of the limb after a time, when no union of the fragments has taken place, if only the patient continues to use the limb, and thus develops the muscles.

M. Velpeau asserts that he has seen the functions of the knee joint "completely re-established, with an interval of two or three inches between the fragments of the patella."

"Such assertions," says M. Malgaigne, " are, in my opinion, only accounted for by some inaccuracy in examination; and for my own part, I have never seen the functions of the limb completely restored, even when the separation was limited to one-third of an inch."

In reference to the cases contained in this and the subsequent reports as treated at Bellevue Hospital it seems proper to say farther, that the House Surgeons who have had the immediate charge of the cases, are almost without exception young men of the highest qualifications.   They secure their positions through a severe concours.   They are careful, attentive and ingenious in devices to accomplish their purposes—they have large experience, and will in all respects compare favorably with the best class of surgeons either at home or abroad.   What difficulties they have experienced, it is fair to say, therefore, will be experienced by other surgeons ; and where they have failed others will fail also.   Of the skill of the distinguished gentlemen who are my colleagues on the visiting staff of Surgeons at Bellevue, it is unnecessary for me to speak, as no one would call it in question.   I desire therefore to repeat, that all of the cases reported as having been under their care, represent in their results the highest standard of excellence yet attained in the treatment of this unfortunate class of accidents.   The same must be said of the few cases reported as having been treated by Surgeons at other city Hospitals and elsewhere, all of whom are personally known to me as men of skill,

FIRST PAPER.

FIFTY-FOUR CASES WHICH HAVE COME UNDER MY OWN OBSERVATION.

SIMPLE, TRANSVERSE FRACTURE, KNOWN TO BE THE RESULT OF A DIRECT FORCE—FIBROUS UNION.

CASE 1.—John McDonald, æt. 22. Fell upon his knee in July, 1859, breaking the right patella below its middle transversely. Dr. I. of Brooklyn, placed his limb upon an inclined plane, and secured it with rollers, &c. It was kept in this position six weeks, after which he began to walk. I examined his leg March 15, 1860, about nine months after the injury, and found the fragments united by a ligament three-quarters of an inch in length. He could not flex the knee more than 15°, yet the limb was strong and serviceable.

CASE 2.—Ed. Fitzgibbons, æt. 25, residing at 151 Navy Street, Brooklyn. Was kicked upon his left knee January 10, 1865 or '66 and admitted to Dr. Sayre's ward, Bellevue Hospital.

I took charge of him February 1, '65, when the service reverted to me. I found the limb dressed and supported upon my single inclined plane, the fragments being separated half an inch. Fibrous union.

CASE 3.—Mrs. Valorus Hodges, æt, 53. Fell upon her knee February 5, 1860, breaking the left patella transversely near its middle. The fragments were separated one inch. On the seventh day I applied a long, straight splint to the back of the limb, carefully fitted and padded, raised the lower end of the splint eight inches, and elevated the shoulders; securing the fragments as well as possible in place by a roller. This brought the fragments together within half an inch. A fibrous union resulted.

CASE 4.—Henry G. Van Hotten, æt. 22. Fell upon his left knee March 12, 1856, breaking it transversely. It was treated by a surgeon in Paterson, N. J. Mr. V. says it was kept in a splint more than one year, and that it was five months more before he had the use of his knee-joint.

November 18, 1863.—I found the fragments separated one inch, and united by ligaments. He walked well, and was serving in the U. S. Infantry as a common soldier.

CASES 5 & 6.—(Both patellæ) John Dundas, æt. 22. Fell, Oct. 22, 1852, while asleep, from the third story of a dwelling house striking his knees upon the stone sidewalk, and breaking *both patellæ* transversely.

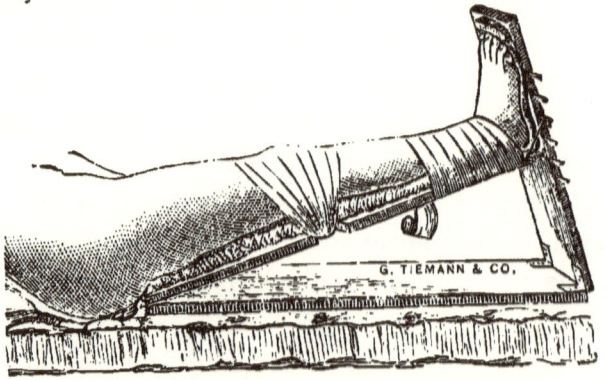

Hamilton's single inclined plane for fractures of the patella.
FIG. I.

Two surgeons took him in charge, and applied two long thigh and leg splints. On the tenth day he was sent to the Buffalo Hospital of the Sisters of Charity, and came under my charge. My inclined plane apparatus was applied, adhesive plasters were laid obliquely above and below the patellæ to secure apposition or approximation of the fragments, and the limbs bound to the apparatus with rollers saturated with flour paste.

On the 37th day the dressings were removed and not re-applied. Both patellæ had united by ligaments of half an inch in length.

CASE 7.—John Williams æt. 26. Fell in 1869, breaking the left patella transversely. Admitted to Bellevue, ward 11.

I returned to duty March 1, 1870, and removed his splint March 3. He had been in the hospital with the splint continuously upon the limb three months and eight days. The fragments were united with a ligament three-quarters of an inch in length. The knee-joint was almost completely anchylosed.

CASE 8.—Edward Vedder, æt. 45. Was struck by a horse car, Sept. 25th, 1874, and taken to the Centre Street Hospital, where a posterior leg splint was applied.

Sept. 30.—Brought to Bellevue, 3d Surg. Division, my service. Found he had a transverse fracture of the patella; fragments separated one-half inch; knee swollen. A splint was secured to the limb, with a figure-of-eight bandage, about the knee, and the foot elevated.

Oct. 7.—Adhesive plasters "locked" over patella; figure-of-eight to knee and a plaster-of-Paris bandage from the ankle to the middle of the thigh.

Oct. 24.—29 days, splint removed. Fibrous union, one-half inch in length. Simple long splint.

Nov. 8.—Removed. 12th, on crutches.

Dec. 7.—Considerable power of flexion. Can walk some without crutches.

Dec. 19.—Discharged.

CASE 9.—Samuel McEvitt, æt. 62. Slipped on the sidewalk March 17th, 1879, striking upon and breaking the left patella. The upper third of the bone was broken off. He did not know it was broken. A surgeon was called on the third day, and said it was not broken. Hot fomentations were applied, and until the 16th day after the accident he was in bed or upon the sofa, going from the one to the other without aid, except from a cane.

Admitted to ward 30, Bellevue, April 2, 1879. Knee swollen. Hot fomentations applied. Fragments separated about three-quarters of an inch.

The limb was dressed April 3d, the 17th day, with a long posterior, straight splint, retained in place with a bandage saturated with the silicate of soda in solution. Above and below the knee the bandage was carried in the form of the figure-of-eight, a pad of folded cloth being laid above and below the patella, next to the skin.

I came on duty May 1, and May 4th, 46 days after the acci. dent, and 29 after admission, the dressings were for the first time removed. The fragments were found united by ligament. Each fragment could be moved laterally and separately. The upper fragment was drawn up on its inner side five-eighths of an inch, and on its outer margin two-eighths of an inch. It was also displaced inwards about two-eighths of an inch. It could not by pressure be made to resume its natural position. The diameter of both fragments was lengthened half an inch, as if from hypertrophy or expansion of the fragments in the direction of their circumference. The lower edge of the upper fragment was depressed by the overlying pad, and the upper edge of the lower fragment elevated by the pad below.

The anchylosis of the knee was almost, but not quite complete, and all attempts at passive motion were very painful.

A piece of felt, long enough to extend from the middle of the thigh to below the middle of the leg, was now moulded to the back of the limb, covered with flannel cloth and secured in place by a roller. Instructions being given to the House Surgeon, to remove it daily and give to the joint passive motion ; not, however, flexing the limb sufficiently to cause much pain, or to endanger the newly formed ligament. He was permitted to go about on crutches.

June 24th.—Motion of joint a little increased. Felt splint laid aside, and limb left without bandages.

CASE 10.—Luke Cavanagh, æt. 60. Fell on his right knee upon the edge of a stone step, May 22, 1869, breaking the right patella transversely a little below the middle. Intemperate. Admitted to Bellevue Hospital, ward 11, 3rd Surg. Div., May 24.

There was pretty extensive ecchymosis and swelling around the knee. The bursa patella was distended with a fluctuating fluid. The capsule of the joint was also distended moderately. The fragments were apparently in contact, so that crepitus was easily developed.

A straight posterior splint was applied, secured with bandages, the bandages about the knee being laid obliquely above and below the patella.

The patient was very turbulent, and removed the dressings himself repeatedly five or six times.

June 2nd.—He was secured in a straight-jacket. This was removed from him on the 5th. The limb was again dressed on the straight splint, the fragments being supported with adhesive strips laid above and below the patella.

June 28th.—(35 days) firm ligamentous union, of one quarter of an inch. Some anchylosis.

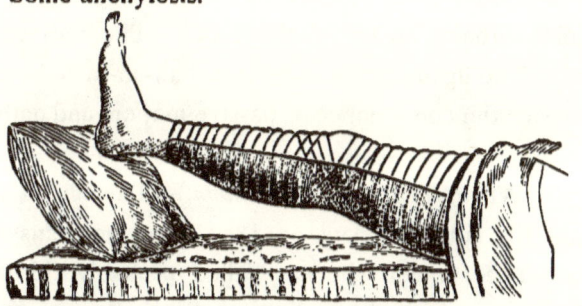

Hamilton's portative, or bed dressing for fractured patella.

FIG. 2.

June 30th.—Went out on pass and did not return.

CASE II.—Mrs. McI—, aged about 40. Fell down a flight of steps outside of her door, striking her left knee upon a stone side-walk, April 23, 1874, breaking the patella transversely a little above its middle. I saw her on the same day. The knee was much bruised and swollen. I applied at once a gutta percha splint made to fit accurately the back and sides of her knee, including considerable portions of the thigh and leg ; and secured the splint with a roller, laying the limb straight upon pillows. The splint was covered with flannel cloth, and the roller was stitched to the cover. (My portative apparatus.) At short intervals subsequently, the splint was removed, and passive motion was practiced very early. The fragments united with a bond of about half-an-inch in length, which felt like bone; it is probably fibrous.

CASE 12.—Miss Ellen Budd, æt. 42, of Hayesville, Ohio. Fell upon frozen ground in April, 1874, breaking the right patella transversely in its lower third. She was placed under the care of Dr. E. V. Kerrdig, of Hayesville. He applied a long straight posterior splint, securing the fragments with adhesive plaster strips. No unusual inflammation or swelling occurred. At the end of four weeks, Dr. K. began to employ passive motion, and in about seven weeks the splint was removed, when the fragments were found to be united with a ligament of half-an-inch in length. The knee could then be flexed about 5°. She has since been using crutches, and when she consulted me, about seven months after the injury, she could move the knee-joint through an arc of about 15°. The limb was slightly œdematous. The ligamentous bond was half-an-inch in length and firm. I advised the continuance of passive motion, and daily exercise in walking.

CASE 13.—(*No apparatus. Good union.*)—Theophilus Alles, æt. 56. Fell on the sidewalk Aug. 27, 1854, breaking transversely the left patella. The surgeon who was called probably did not recognize the fracture, as he only applied a roller. Two weeks later he was placed in one of the wards of the Hospital of the Sisters of Charity, Buffalo, and here, for reasons unknown to me, the same treatment was continued.

Oct. 1, 1854.—When my term of service commenced, five weeks after the accident, I found the fracture united with a ligament of half-an-inch.

CASE 14.—John Delaney, æt. 36. Fell March 7th, 1851, fifteen feet, striking on his knee and breaking the patella transversely. He came under my care two weeks later, when I applied my own apparatus (inclined plane). The fragments united with a ligament one-quarter of an inch in length.

CASE 15.—A laborer, æt. 25, stumbled and fell upon his knee, when running at full speed. He was treated by Dr. Mixer, of

Buffalo, and myself, with my own apparatus—the inclined plane.

Four months after the injury the functions of the limb were completely restored, the fragments having united with a ligament half an inch in length.

CASE 16.—Catharine McGloughlin, æt. 30, fell from a window, breaking the left patella in a transverse direction from side to side, but somewhat curved downwards in its middle. She received also severe injuries about her head and side. On the sixth day she was taken to the Presbyterian Hospital in this city, and remained there five months. During the first eight weeks she had a posterior splint upon the leg. Then a plaster-of-Paris splint was applied, which she wore a few weeks. About two months before she called upon me, she had a knee-cap applied, and has worn it to the present time.

August 26th, 1879, nine months after the injury, I examined the limb. The fragments were separated half an inch, and united by a firm fibrous band. The upper fragment was slightly and the lower fragment very much hypertrophied, especially in its transverse diameter. She could flex her leg only to a right angle, but she could extend it fully. In descending or ascending steps she was obliged to put the sound limb first. She experienced almost constant pain in the region of the inner part of the lower fragment. The muscles of the left hip and thigh were much wasted. She was unable to work, and prayed that something might be done to stop the pain.

I advised that the knee-cap be discontinued, and that she apply hot water to the limb daily. The latter she had already done with some relief, at the suggestion of Dr. Gibney, of the Hospital for the Ruptured and Crippled.

SIMPLE TRANSVERSE FRACTURE—DIRECT FORCE—FIBROUS UNION—
RUPTURE OF LIGAMENT.

CASE 17.—Michael Taylor, æt. 38. Fell while running, April 18, 1869, striking upon his left knee and breaking the patella transversely. He was admitted to the Long Island College Hospital, and the limb was dressed upon my single inclined plane. The fracture united with a short ligament, but on the 22d of May, about five weeks after the fracture occurred, he left the hospital without permission, and ruptured the ligament.   I have no knowledge of the case after this.

CASE 18.—Patrick O'Hara, æt. 39.   Broke his right patella, Sept. 18, 1876, by a fall upon his knee.   Taken to Quarantine Hospital, (Drs. O'Dea and Anderson;) was in hospital three months, with posterior splint and adhesive plasters in form of the "lock strap." After being discharged, joint was rather stiff, but could walk and work.

Jan. 17th, 1879.—While walking stumbled and his leg bent under him to an acute angle, refracturing the ligament.   Taken to Chambers St. Hospital, and the following day to Bellevue—service of Dr. Darby.   Swollen and inflamed.   Icebags applied and continued two weeks, then Dr. Morrow applied plaster-of-Paris.   Staid in bed two weeks, and was then on crutches two weeks.   At end of eight weeks splint removed and a plaster-of-Paris splint applied, open in front.

About the 7th of April was discharged, and he wore the splint two weeks longer.   Has been walking ever since.

Aug. 13th, 1879.—Fragments separated 2¼ inches when the leg is straight, and 3½ when it is bent ; it bends only to a right angle. The lower fragment is wider than natural.   He walks well on a level surface, but has to put the sound leg first in going up stairs.   I cannot feel any ligament between the fragments; the articulating surface of the femur being distinctly felt.

CASE 19.—Dr. H. C. B., of Crawford Co., Pa., æt. 19.   Fell upon a stone in March, 1859, breaking the right patella transversely a little below its middle.   A neighboring surgeon dressed the limb first with a roller.   He then placed the limb upon a straight splint in a nearly horizontal position.   It was kept in this position three months, being, however, occasionally exposed and rubbed.   At this time it had united by a ligament of about half or three quarters of an inch in length. The knee was then quite stiff.   As soon as he began to use the limb the upper fragment commenced to draw up gradually, and at the end of a year it was separated three inches and a half.

I examined him in 1865, about six years after the accident. The upper fragment was separated three and a half inches, the same as at the end of the first year. There is only a long narrow ligament on the inside of the patella, in which a new patella has formed, one inch long by half an inch in thickness. The motions of the joint are free, and he walks without a halt. Long walks, however, fatigue this leg more than the other.

CASE 20.—Abraham Sackett, æt. 58. Fell upon his left knee, upon a railroad iron, January 22, 1872, breaking the patella transversely near its middle. The fragments were at once separated four and a half inches.

It was treated by Dr. John Nolan, of this city. My apparatus—the inclined plane—was employed, and the fragments secured with adhesive strips This was continued nearly eleven weeks, when the fragments were found united with a ligature of one quarter of an inch in length. He then began to walk with crutches and had a pretty good leg. Five months later he was thrown from a carriage and ruptured the ligament.

When he consulted me, October 3, 1873, nearly four years after the injury, the upper fragment was separated two inches from the lower. He could flex and extend the leg, and could walk tolerably well. Dr. Nolan informs me that he subsequently wore an elastic knee-cap. He is now dead.

CASE 21.—Mary Gorley, æt. 40. Fell in the street September 28, 1870, and on the same day admitted to Bellevue, 3d Surg. Div.

There was a transverse fracture below the middle, with a separation of two inches. Knee swollen, and considerable ecchymosis in popliteal space.

She stated that she had fallen on the ice four years before, and that a bone on the knee " stuck up;" that a doctor was called who put it on an inclined plane for eight weeks, and that she had never since then been able to straighten the knee. (The presumption is that there was a fracture of the patella.)

The hospital record states that I saw the patient October 3, 1870

fifth day after last accident.   The swelling was mostly gone, and a
posterior leather splint was applied (my portative apparatus.)

November 3.—Thirty-six days after accident—walking on crutches,
makes no attempt to use the limb.   Sent to Charity Hospital.   She
was discharged from Charity Hospital February 4, 1871.   Result not
known.

SIMPLE TRANSVERSE FRACTURE—DIRECT FORCE—NO UNION.

CASE 22.—Samuel Hanna, æt. 38.   Fell upon the ice in December,
1871, striking upon his left knee and breaking the patella transversely about its middle.

I found Hanna in my ward at Bellevue, June 1, 1875, admitted on
account of an abscess which had formed without any appreciable
cause in the areolar tissue, just above the left knee.   He had an old
fracture of the patella in the same limb, the fragments being separated nearly four inches.   He was unable to extend the limb by
muscular action, there being apparently no bond of union between
the fragments.

He gave the following account of the injury: The accident occurred
as stated above in December, 1871, about three years and five months
before.   He was immediately taken to Bellevue Hospital.   On the
fourth day the limb was laid upon an inclined plane.   On about the
seventh day a plaster-of-Paris splint was applied from the foot to the
hip.   He was permitted to go about on crutches.   When the splint
was removed the fragments were separated two inches.   He has had
no treatment for the fracture since.

CASE 23.—John Sharkie, æt. 24, a soldier in the British service.
Was struck on the right knee while he was sitting with his leg bent
under him.

He was immediately put under charge of the surgeon of the 89th
regiment of infantry.   Severe inflammation and swelling ensued, and
no apparatus was employed until the twelfth day, a compress was
then laid over both fragments, and they were bound on with a roller,
the limb being laid upon an inclined plane.   The bandages were

removed at the end of four months, when the upper fragment at once drew up toward the body. It was eighteen months before he could walk without a cane. This is the account given to me by himself.

Twenty-nine years after the accident, March 27, 1855, I found when the limb was straight, that the upper fragment lay two and a half inches above the lower, and when the limb was flexed it separated five inches. No trace of a ligament or other bond of union could be felt. He walks well, without a cane, there being very little or no halt, but he cannot walk fast.

SIMPLE TRANSVERSE FRACTURE—DIRECT BLOW—RESULT UNKNOWN.

CASE 24.—John Mooney, æt. 63. Fell Jan. 17, 1873, striking on his right patella and breaking it transversely near its middle. He was received at the Park Reception Hospital on the same day. Dr. Fluhrer, the House Surgeon, applied a straight, flat, posterior splint. Six days later I found the fragments separated one inch, and directed a long leather splint to be substituted, fitted accurately to the back of the limb, covered with woolen cloth, and secured to the limb with bandages. The bandages being laid obliquely above and below the fragments, and the whole being stitched to the cover of the splint (my portative apparatus).

CASE 25.—Thomas Barker, æt. 30. While walking April 9, 1874, his left foot turned under him, and he fell upon the flagging, striking on the same knee. He was unable to rise.

On the same day he was taken to Bellevue, 3d Surg. Div., my service, and was found to have a transverse fracture of the left patella.

April 10.—A plaster-of-Paris splint was applied, the roller covering the patella in the form of a figure-of-8.

April 30.—21st day, discharged.

(No farther record of the case. He probably left with a promise to return.)

SIMPLE TRANSVERSE FRACTURE—DIRECT FORCE—COMPLICATED WITH OTHER INJURIES—DEATH.

CASE 26.—Mrs. Catherine Sullivan, æt. 55. Fell through a hatch-way, Oct. 9, 1866, breaking the right thigh and right patella. The patella was broken transversely. The fracture of the thigh was just above the knee and compound. She was admitted to ward 15, 3d Surg. Div., my service, on the same day, and amputation was advised.

This she refused to have made. Sufficient permanent extension was applied to steady the limb, and an attempt was made to save her life, but on the 30th of October she had a chill. Chills continued to occur at intervals until the 3d of Nov., when she died.

SIMPLE TRANSVERSE FRACTURE KNOWN TO BE THE RESULT OF MUS-CULAR ACTION—FIBROUS UNION.

CASE 27.—Dan'l Gary, æt. 24. Fell Jan. 26, 1873, and in the attempt to save himself, felt the left patella break. Admitted to Bellevue on same day. Patient has had morbus coxæ in the right limb since childhood. The fragments of the broken patella were brought together with broad adhesive strips laid longitudinally above and below the knee, and "locked" in front. The limb was secured to a straight splint. The whole being enclosed in a plaster-of-Paris splint.

FIG. 3.—LOCK STRAP.

Feb'y 5th.—Dressings removed. Apposition of fragments said to be perfect. Substituted starch bandage for the plaster-of-Paris, reinforced with long, narrow strips of zinc, laid longitudinally. Re-applied the adhesive strips as before.

Feb'y 12th.—Removed all dressings. Apposition said to be perfect. Substituted plaster-of-Paris, with zinc strips, for starch.

Feb'y 25th.—For the fourth time splint reapplied.

March 10th.—Splint reapplied for the fifth time. Fragments united firmly. Apposition said to be perfect.

May 30th.—Ninety-seven days, or about fourteen weeks, after the injury, I found this patient in my service (my service having commenced on the 1st of May.) The apparatus was removed, and the union was found to be effected by a ligament of one-quarter of an inch in length—slight motion at the knee-joint.

May 15th.—Motion increased. Discharged.

CASE 28.—Joseph Cox, æt. 50. Slipped on ice and broke the right patella in the effort to recover himself while falling backwards. This occurred in Jan., 1875 ; he was carried home because he could not stand. Had no pain, and did not suspect the fracture until he reached home and was seated in a chair, when he noticed a space between the fragments of about one and a half inches. It was not tender to the touch. He put them together himself, and made them grate. It was a good deal swollen when he reached home.

For three days he sat with his leg on a chair, or walked about with a cane. Meanwhile it continued to swell. On third day sent for Dr. ———, who elevated the leg, and on the following day applied my inclined plane apparatus, supporting the fragments with oblique adhesive strips. I saw the case in consultation about three weeks later.

Apparatus kept on six weeks, when (not by my advice) a plaster-of-Paris splint was applied, and he was allowed to go about with crutches.

Dr. John Nolan was called when the plaster had been on about one week. Meanwhile the foot had become swollen, purple, being threatened with gangrene, and the limb was very painful, so that Mr. Cox had himself cut the splint nearly off to get relief.

Dr. Nolan put him again on my inclined plane, with adhesive strips, and in about three weeks a fibrous union had taken place of about three-quarters of an inch in length. Soon after it was removed the fibrous band began to lengthen.

By courtesy of Dr. Nolan I saw the patient again, July 27, 1879. The fracture is transverse through the middle. The fragments are separated one and a half inches; both fragments are a little hypertrophied, but the lower one is the most; it being one-half inch wider than the sound patella. Lower fragments tilted forwards. There is a strong fibrous union, but on the inner side it has given way some, and allowed the upper fragment to turn upon its axis. He can straighten the leg completely while sitting, and can flex nearly to a right angle. The motions are accompanied with a clicking sensation. He walks with ease, and naturally, but in descending steps he is obliged to put the left foot down first. He bears no more weight upon the sound limb than upon the opposite. He thinks the ligament continued to stretch until about one year ago.

SIMPLE TRANSVERSE FRACTURE FROM MUSCULAR ACTION.—FIBROUS UNION.

CASE 29.—Miss C., æt. 40. Tripped and fell Feb. 1, 1870, and in the attempt to recover herself broke the right patella transversely. The fracture was about half an inch above its lower end. It was treated by Dr. W. V. White, of this city, upon a single inclined plane, according to my method.

Five weeks after the injury I saw the patient with Dr. White. The fragments were united by a ligament one-quarter of an inch in length. The dressing was continued a week longer, passive motion being employed occasionally. She walked about the house a little in April and May. The following autumn she wrote to Dr. White that she was almost entirely well. The only difficulty she experienced was in going up and down stairs.

CASE 30.—Bridget Regan, æt. 34. Fell Nov. 22, 1868, but recovered herself and did not touch the ground, breaking the left patella transversely. The fragments became at once separated four or five inches. She was sent to Charity Hospital and under my care my own apparatus was applied.

On returning to my service I found her, Feb. 3, 1869, seventy-three days after the injury, still upon the same apparatus. I removed the dressing and found the patella united by a ligament of half an inch in length. Knee-joint almost motionless. This extreme anchylosis was due probably to the long confinement, but for this I was not responsible. I have no farther notes of the case, and do not know the final result

CASE 31.—Through the courtesy of Dr. Francis V. White, of this city, I have been permitted to see the following case treated by himself, and published, in connection with a valuable paper on fracture of the patella, in the *Medical Record*, July 1st and 15th, 1867.

Mrs. R., æt. 41, a rather fleshy woman, broke her left patella above its middle, July 11, 1860, from muscular action.

Dr. White applied Turner's apparatus on the third day, his intention being "to obtain bony union." This apparatus is essentially a back splint with an arrangement by which the adhesive strips laid above and below the fragments and obliquely around the splint, may be tightened from time to time by the action of a screw. This was worn sixty-nine days, and sixty-eight days later "the patella appeared united by bone." Careful passive motion was employed at intervals during the treatment, which continued to the 28th of Nov., not quite five months. Before dismissal, he "had the patient occasionally sit on a table, and swing the leg." When Dr. White examined the limb about five months later he found a *fibrous* union of about half an inch in length. It is evident, therefore, that it was not bony when Dr. White supposed it to be; and this erroneous conclusion has probably often been made.

I examined Mrs. R. carefully in presence of Dr. White, August 4th, 1879, nineteen years after the injury. Mrs. R. is still rather stout, and in good health. The upper fragment is separated from the lower, when she extends the leg, about half an inch, and when she flexes it about three-quarters of an inch.

The fragments are of normal size, the lower—the larger—being very slightly tilted forward at its upper margin. She can flex and extend the leg as perfectly as the other, and walks up and down stairs without a cane as naturally and as easily as any other person. She says, however, that she did not attain this perfection until about two years after the accident. Moving the lower fragment upwards causes a chafing, as if there was an absence of the synovial membrane, but this causes no pain.

Dr. White experienced some difficulty in preventing excoriations of the skin where the adhesive plaster crossed the limb above and below the fragments, precisely as others have experienced ; nor could the patient walk about with the apparatus without considerable inconvenience. In short, while the apparatus seems to have answered its purpose as well as most other forms of dressing, the inventor cannot claim to accomplish more than can be accomplished by others ; no bony union has resulted, the ligament has the average length, the patient was as long under treatment as others; but what interests us especially is that, after two years, the use of the limb is in all respects perfect. We cannot see, however, what special connection there is between this fact and the form of apparatus employed in the case under consideration.

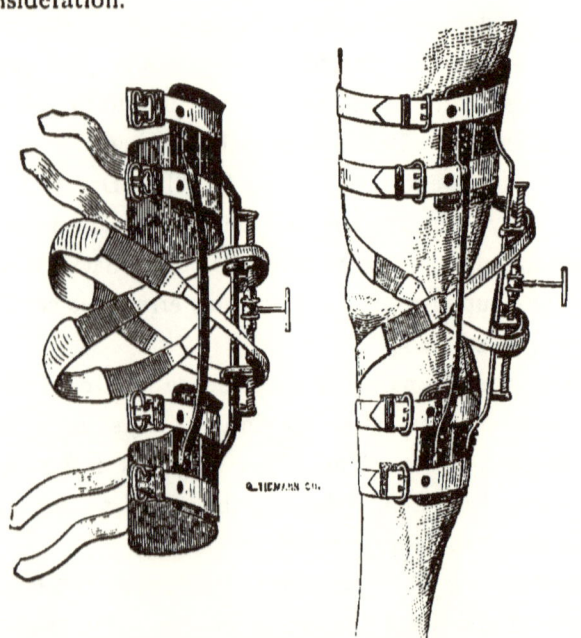

Turner's apparatus for fracture of the patella.

CASE 32.—Martin Geiger, æt. 23. About eleven months ago slipped and fell backwards, breaking the left patella transversely.

He felt it give way ; could not stand. Same day taken to New York Hospital. On the following day the limb was placed on an inclined plane, with bandages, etc. The knee was swollen. About four weeks later a plaster-of-Paris splint applied. Next day removed a section of splint of about four inches in width, from the upper to the lower end, placed pads above and below fragments, and with adhesive strips, a buckle, etc., drew the fragments together from day to day. This was kept on about three weeks, a part of which time he was on crutches. Then a silicate of soda splint was applied to the entire leg and thigh, and he was permitted to go about on crutches. Subsequently this was removed and a new one applied. After being in the hospital about sixteen or seventeen weeks he was discharged, a flannel bandage still on the limb. Soon after he went to the Hospital for Ruptured and Crippled, where an elastic knee-cap was applied, which enabled him to walk better.

By courtesy of Dr. Gibney, I examined the limb August 18, 1879, about eleven months after the injury. The fracture was transverse, and a little above its middle. Fragments separated 1½ inches on the inner side, and ½ inch on the outer side. The muscles of the thigh are atrophied, the circumference of the limb being three inches less than the opposite. He cannot flex the leg completely, and he has to walk very carefully, as leg gives way easily. He has no power to straighten the knee when he is sitting, and the leg is flexed. It has not improved for some time past. When he left the hospital he could only move the joint very little. The fragments move freely, and a ligament can be felt distinctly on the outer side, but not on the inner. I advised discontinuance of the knee-cap.

CASE 33.—J. H., fireman, æt. 39. In descending a flight of steps rapidly, April 10th, 1879, fell, and in his effort to recover himself, without striking the ground, he felt the patella give way with a snap.

He was immediately brought to Bellevue, 4th Surg. Div. The knee was found swollen, and very painful. Fracture transverse, and below the middle. Crepitus. Icebags applied, and later a long posterior splint and a snug bandage from the toes up.

April 15.—Ice-bags and dressings continued until to-day. Swelling nearly gone. Considerable ecchymosis on sides of knee and back of thigh. A padded splint applied, ten inches broad, and extending beyond the foot.   This was firmly bandaged to the leg, and, in order to bring the fragments together, bands of adhesive plaster encircled the limb completely a few inches above and below the knee: these serving as a basis, to the front of which were attached an elastic band and buckle, with pads underneath.   Within two hours after this was buckled it was so painful that it had to be loosened.   He received a subcutaneous injection of morphine, which was repeated in the evening.

April 16.—Strap and buckle tightened about the 25th of an inch.

April 18.—Tightened two-thirds of an inch.   For sleeplessness ordered chlorate hydrate, gr. xv.

April 20.—Apparatus removed and re-applied.   Adhesive strips, form of figure-of-8, substituted for buckles and straps.

April 21.—Suffered great pain after last dressing.   " Thought leg would burst."   Apparatus removed and re-applied after more neat adjustment of fragments.

April 22.—Dressings disarranged.   Removed and re-applied.   Complains of pain in his foot.   Ordered: morphine, U. S. sol., ℥ j.

April 23.—Dressings removed on account of the pain, and re-applied.   U. S. sol., morph., ℥ ss., in the morning, and 10 m. Majendie, sol. hypodermically at night.

April 27.—Ice-bags still continued.

April 28.—A long, straight board splint, padded, was laid upon the back of the leg and thigh.   This was secured in place by plaster-of-Paris bandages, extending from the toes to the middle of the thigh, except that an interval or opening of about six inches was left over the knee and on the sides.   A broad strap of webbing, furnished with a buckle, was made fast to the thigh by the aid of circular adhesive plasters placed above and below, to be buckled in front of the knee. Four pads were then placed upon the knee, namely, one above the patella, one below, and two in front; over these the strap was buckled, and the whole knee covered in by circular and reversed turns of a roller.   The patient was now placed upon a bed, with the foot of the injured limb somewhat elevated.

My hospital service re-commenced May 1.—*May* 3 (about twenty-two days after the injury was received).—I examined the fracture, and found the fragments separated half an inch; the lower fragments being displaced inwards about half an inch, and it could not be restored to its position by force. There was slight lateral motion in the upper fragment.

The apparatus was permitted to remain, except that a pad, which had become displaced probably, and rested directly over the point of separation between the two fragments, was removed. It had caused a depression, and was likely to prevent the formation of the ligament. A pad was placed on the inner margin of the lower fragment, with straps to displace it outwards. This was found to be ineffective, and was removed on the 13th.

May 15.—Thirty-five days after the accident, and nineteen after the immovable apparatus was applied, the whole apparatus was removed, and my portative felt splint substituted.

At this time a careful examination of the limb was made, and the fragments were found separated and displaced as on the 3d of May, that is, separated half an inch, and the lower fragment displaced inwards half an inch. The space between the fragments felt firm, as if a ligament had formed. The upper fragment could not be moved up or down, nor could it be disturbed by the action of his muscles in rising or lying down in bed. The patella was enlarged in all its diameters, half an inch. The splint was directed to be removed daily, and passive motion employed very carefully. He was permitted to go about upon crutches, and he was especially directed to keep his toes lifted by suspension from the shoulder, it being noticed that they were inclined to fall into a state of passive extension.

May 30.—All apparatus removed and not re-applied, and it was now discovered that the toes fell in consequence of paralysis ; the paralysis extending to most or all of the extensor muscles, and perhaps to some others.

In addition to elevating the toes by suspension from the shoulders, he was directed to make frequent efforts to move the toes, the electrical current was employed and also alternate douches of hot and cold water. Still later strychnine was injected hypodermically, $\frac{1}{48}$th of a grain, *ter die*, and stimulating embrocations employed.

July 17.—Has the power of moving one or two of his toes a little, and a favorable prognosis is made.

The anchylosis of the knee is diminished. The lateral displacement of the lower fragment has also nearly disappeared; its restoration seeming to be accomplished by the traction of the new ligament.

Sept. 6.—Still in the hospital—paralysis continues only in extensors of great toe.

CASE 34.—A sailor was thrown backwards, breaking the patella transversely. He came under my charge on the third day. My apparatus (inclined plane) was applied, and in four weeks the fragments were united by ligament, with a separation of half an inch.

CASE 35.—Mary Conolly, æt. 32. Fell February 15, 1876, breaking the left patella transversely. She does not know how she struck. Taken same night to Chambers St. Hospital. She says no splint was applied, but her account of the treatment at this hospital is not very reliable, except that she says the fragments were drawn together by adhesive strips laid longitudinally.

She was admitted to Bellevue, March 27th, where, under my instruction, a leather splint was moulded to the back of her leg, covered with woolen cloth and secured in place by rollers; the rollers being carried in the form of a figure-of-8 above and below the knee.

May 3.—About five weeks after admission, the splint was removed, and the fragments found united by a ligament half an inch in length. Considerable motion in joint. The splint ordered to be removed daily and the joint moved carefully.

CASE 36.—Edward Laffey, æt. 20. Fractured right patella transversely, Oct. 24, 1851. Dr. Shaw, of Silver Creek, N. Y., dressed the limb with Sir Astley Cooper's apparatus (*see my Treatise on Fractures and Dislocations, 5th Ed. p.* 469.)

Nov. 1.—He came under my care, and the same dressings were continued to Nov. 26, when my own apparatus was substituted. This also was removed Dec. 5th, forty-one days from the day of the injury.

The fragments had united by a ligament one-quarter of an inch in length.

CASE 37.—Miles Griffin, æt. 47. Admitted to Bellevue March, 1871, with a simple transverse fracture, about the middle of the right patella.

Dressed with plaster-of-Paris bandage.

I saw the limb when it had been eight weeks in the splint. Fragments united by a ligament half an inch in length. Almost complete anchylosis.

SIMPLE TRANSVERSE FRACTURE FROM MUSCULAR ACTION—FIBROUS
UNION—RUPTURE OF LIGAMENT.

CASE 38.—Sarah Vibbett, æt. 27. Fell while walking, Nov. 24, 1874. She felt the bone break before she struck the ground, and she was unable to straighten her leg. She was taken to the Park Reception Hospital, Dr. Fluhrer in charge. A plaster-of-Paris splint was applied on the same day. She left the hospital in four weeks, and four weeks later the splint was removed. She says the knee-joint was then perfectly immovable, and that she could lay her thumb between the fragments (union by ligament of, probably, half or three quarters of an inch). In February, 1875, about one month after the splint was removed, she fell again, and then found the fragments had been separated three inches.

April 22.—About five months after the first accident, and about two months after the second, she was in Dr. Erskine Mason's service at Bellevue, and through his courtesy I was permitted to see her. I found the upper fragment separated from the lower three inches while the leg was straight, but when flexed it ascended four inches. By keeping the leg carefully under the centre of gravity she could walk slowly, moving the toes forward and backwards by the action of the muscles about two inches.

Dr. Mason has applied a knee-cap and does not propose to do anything more.

CASE 39.—A. T. Smith, Davenport, Ohio. In jumping from a carriage, Nov. 23, 1874, broke the patella of the right leg, transversely and below the middle. Caused by muscular action, as his knee did not strike the ground. Dr. Maxwell, of Davenport, was called. The fragments were separated, when the leg was straight, half an inch, and when flexed one inch. Dr. Maxwell applied a splint made of binders' board, and moulded to the back of the limb, straight; and secured this with figure-of-8 bandages about the knee, and with circular bandages at other points. This was worn about three months, he being permitted most of the time to go about. When finally removed the fragments seemed to be well united by ligament, "with only a little separation on the inside." From this time the ligament has been gradually giving way, and when he consulted me, February 28, 1876, about fifteen months after the injury, I found the fragments separated three inches. The muscles of the thigh were small. He could not straighten the leg completely by muscular action, but he walked slowly without any appreciable halt. I advised continued use of the limb and daily use of the battery.

CASE 40.—Asst. Surg. T. D. Myers, U. S. Navy, æt. 29. Broke his right patella May 19, 1874, when returning from the U. S. Ship, Kearsarge, from muscular action in attempting to save himself from a fall. The fracture was transverse, and below the middle—at the upper end of the lower fourth. The fragments at once separated fully four and a half inches. Surgeon Bloodgood in charge. May 21, he was sent to the hospital at Yokohama. A long posterior splint was applied and the fragments secured with a figure-of-8 bandage. May 24th, Lausdale's apparatus (see fig. 216, p. 472, fifth Ed. of my work on Fractures and Dislocations) was applied. This was worn five days, when it was found to have caused a slight ulceration above the upper fragment, and it was removed. A straight splint, secured at the knee by adhesive strips, was substituted, and kept on several weeks, and soon after he began to walk, the fragments being united by a ligament one half an inch in length on the inside, and one quarter of an inch on the outside.

Aug. 2nd, 1874.—Seventy-five days after the first injury was received, and not long after he began to walk, he slipped and broke it again from muscular action. He was still in the hospital at Yokahama. A plaster-of-Paris splint was now applied, which was renewed once in about eight days, and finally removed at the end of eight weeks. While this splint was on the limb he was allowed to go about on crutches. On removal it was found that no union of any kind had taken place. From this time forwards, a period of over five months and two weeks he has supported the limb with a leather splint and has walked about on crutches or with a cane.

Asst. Surgeon Myers consulted me March 17th, 1875. I found the fragments separated four and a half inches with very little motion at the knee-joint. Could not detect any bond of union. Advised the removal of the leather splint, and a daily use of the limb by passive motion and active exercise in walking, electricity, shampooing, &c.

In a letter from Asst. Surgeon Myers, dated May 23d, 1875, he says : " Since consulting you March 17th, 1875, I have steadily pursued the plan of treatment suggested by you," &c. " The functions of the limb have gradually returned, till now I am able to walk very well, with very little or no limping." * * " The atrophy of the muscles is gradually disappearing." * * and he concludes with expressions of gratitude for the happy result of the change in the mode of treatment. (For a more full account of this case see *Buffalo Med. Jour.*, Sept. 1879.)

SIMPLE TRANSVERSE FRACTURE—EXACT CAUSE UNKNOWN—FIBROUS UNION.

CASE 41.—James McCuen, æt. 33. Fractured the left patella transversely. Dr. Mixer, of Buffalo, and myself in attendance. We employed a straight splint and roller. Dressings were continued three weeks and three days.

I examined this limb two years later and found the patella united by a ligament half an inch long. The leg was not quite as strong as the opposite.

SIMPLE TRANSVERSE FRACTURE—EXACT CAUSE UNKNOWN—FIBROUS

UNION—RUPTURE OF LIGAMENT.

CASE 42.—James T., æt 28. Fractured his left patella in 1862. It
united by a short ligament which was subsequently ruptured by a fall.
Jan., 1866, while an inmate of Bellevue Hospital, I examined his leg
and found the upper fragment separated from the lower three inches
and a half, in which position it was fixed immovably. He wore
habitually a leather splint made fast against the back of the knee-
joint, and with this he was able to walk. After the original fracture,
which was probably from a direct blow, suppuration ensued, involving the knee-joint, but this left no anchylosis ; the motions of the
joint being free.

CASE 43.—R. J. Donohue, æt. 50. Admitted to Bellevue Hospital.
Feb. 16, 1866, 1st Surgical Div., ward 10. He stated that about eight
weeks before he broke the right patella.

It was treated by a surgeon in the city and united with a short ligament. Four or five weeks later he sat down upon a stone and on
attempting to rise he felt the ligament give way. When admitted the
fragments were separated one inch and ununited. We placed him
upon an inclined plane apparatus and drew down the upper fragment
by adhesive plaster, laid obliquely over leg and splint. The apparatus was removed March 15th, and the fragments were found to have
united with a ligament one-quarter of an inch in length. April 1, he
was discharged.

CASE 44.—Wheeler, æt. 40. Fractured transversely. The fracture
was treated by Dr. Williams. I examined the knee nine weeks after
the fracture occurred. The patient says that the dressing was removed at the end of four weeks, and one week later he began to
walk, but that he almost immediately felt the ligament tear or give
way on the inner side.

I found the ligament unusually short on the outer side, the fragments being apparently in contact, but they were separated one-quarter of an inch on the inner side. The patella was considerably en-

larged in its circumference, as if it had become hypertrophied or had received a new deposit of bone around its margins.

CASE 45.—Michael Fox, æt. 24. Fell Jan. 1, 1876, breaking the right patella transversely.

This man had the foot of the same leg amputated five months before, in consequence of a railroad injury. After the fracture of the patella he was brought to Bellevue, and a plaster-of-Paris splint was applied. Union took place with a ligament.

June 13, 1876.—Five months and two weeks after the first fracture he fell and ruptured the ligament. Admitted to ward 30 (my service.) The limb was much swollen. Fragments separated three inches. I applied a leather splint, moulded to the back of the limb, covered with flannel, and secured the fragments with bandages, circular and oblique (no farther record).

CASE 46.—Carl Abend, æt. 30. Broke his left patella December 4, 1850. Under treatment it united, and on the sixty-first day after the fracture occurred he accidentally ruptured the ligament, and was admitted to the Buffalo Hospital of the Sisters of Charity three days later. I found a transverse fracture with the fragments separated one inch. The whole limb œdematous ; and as the limb had been confined to the splint most of the time since the fracture, I directed it to be left free, and to be bathed twice a day with cold water, and to be rubbed.

Ten days after admission, seventy-four days after the fracture, and thirteen after the rupture, the limb was laid upon and secured to my inclined plane splint. Four weeks later all dressings were removed and the fragments were found united with a ligament of one quarter of an inch in length.

CASE 47.—G. S., male, æt. 35. Fell Dec. 7th, 1878, breaking (probably) his right patella; whether from muscular action or direct force is uncertain. A "bone-setter" saw him, and for three weeks he remained at home with a roller on his leg, not knowing that it was broken. He then went to work, with the roller still on. About eight weeks after the first accident, he met with a second slight accident, and one week

later consulted Dr. John A. Wyeth of this city. Dr. W. found a transverse fracture; the fragments separated one inch, and no union. Dr.
W. brought the fragments together with adhesive strips and applied
a plaster-of-Paris dressing. The next day he walked about. Three
weeks later the splint was removed, passive motion employed, and the
plaster splint reapplied. At the end of six weeks it was finally removed. There was fibrous union of ½ inch in length. Five days
later he slipped and broke it again. The fragments were now separated 3 inches. Finding that none of the ordinary means sufficed to
keep the fragments together, Dr. W. had the following instrument con-
structed and applied:

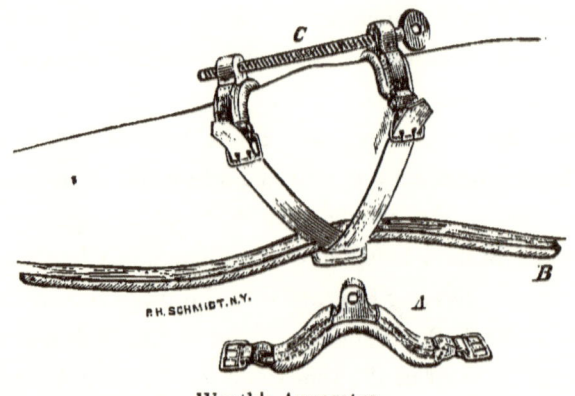

Wyeth's Apparatus.

Fig. 5.

This instrument was removed at the end of twenty-four hours, and
the plaster-of-Paris splint again applied, with a fenestra over the patella. Between the fragments Dr. W. then injected, following the
experiment of Ollier and Goujon, fresh marrow cells. No result except a fibrous union. (*See Medical Record, May* 11, 1878, *for a full
report of this interesting case*).

By courtesy of Dr. Wyeth, I saw this man Aug. 26, 1879, nearly
nine months after the original injury.

The fragments were then separated 1 inch and ⅛ on the outside,
and 1 inch and ¼ on the inside. He could extend the leg fully,
but could only flex it 15°. There was considerable grating under

the fragments when they moved. He walked very well on a level surface, but always put the left foot first in ascending or descending. He suffered no pain.

CASE 48.—Mrs. R. W. H., æt. 36, was thrown down in alighting from a Broadway stage, Dec. 9, 1878, causing a simple transverse fracture of the right patella. She cannot say whether she struck the knee or not ; there was no abrasion of the skin. A surgeon was called immediately, and within one hour after the accident a plaster-of-Paris splint was applied, extending from the toes to the middle of the thigh, but not covering the heel. Three days after, vesicles had formed upon the heel, and it became necessary to open the splint from the toes to a point above the ankle.

Feb. 3, 1879.—Splint removed. Fragments united by a short ligament, and very little mobility of knee-joint, a roller was applied, and after five days more a Tieman's knee-cap was applied. Three weeks after the splint was removed she began to walk on crutches, using also passive motion.

About the 1st of March Mrs. H. discovered that the ligament had stretched, or given way on the inside.

Tieman's Knee-cap.

Fig. 6.

April 11th, 1879.—I saw her in consultation with her surgeon. The fragments were separated on the inner side three-fourths of an inch, and on the outer side one-half inch. The upper fragment is consequently a little tilted. The fracture was transverse, and the upper fragment, constituting one-third of the patella is depressed slightly below the level of the lower. Along the upper margin of the lower fragment there is also a slight crest—probably bony callus—

Both fragments are a little hypertrophied. She says she has not flexed the limb forcibly, and that she did not feel the ligament give way. She walks on a level surface with a cane, and can even walk up and down stairs if she walks slowly and carefully. She can only flex the limb slightly.

SIMPLE OBLIQUE FRACTURE.—DIRECT FORCE.—FIBROUS UNION.

CASE 49.—Margaret Kielt, æt. 67. Fell January 4, 1867, upon her left knee, breaking the patella obliquely downwards and inwards, she was admitted on the same day to Ward 18, Bellevue Hospital. Fragments separated half an inch. My inclined plane apparatus was applied. January 14, fragments separated ¼ inch, and when I went off from duty, Feb. 1, a ligamentous union existed, the fragments being separated half an inch.

Feb. 14th.—All dressings removed.

Feb. 24th.—Knee-joint quite stiff.

Feb. 28th.—Forcible flexion. Posterior adhesions of the patella yielded with a snap. Patella more movable. March 30, passive motion has been continued to date.

She was discharged April 14, 1867, the knee-joint having still only a limited amount of motion.

COMMINUTED FRACTURE.—DIRECT FORCE.—FIBROUS UNION.

CASE 50.—BridgetBrennan, æt. 58. Fell August 31, 1870, upon the sidewalk, striking on her left knee. She was admitted on same day to the 3d Surg. Div., Bellevue—my service. There was. a comminuted fracture, the knee was swollen, and the joint itself inflamed. Tinct. of iodine was applied externally " as a counter irritant! " (Certainly not by my orders).

Sept. 3d.—My own inclined plane apparatus was applied. September 12th, as the position caused pain, the apparatus was removed, and a long posterior leather splint substituted, the fragments being supported by oblique and circular turns of the roller.

Sept. 27th.—27th day—the records say :—" Although union is very poor, the fragments being still separated ¼ of an inch, at her own request she is discharged, still wearing the splint." (I shall congratulate the gentleman who made this record if his average success since he left the hospital has been better than this.)

CASE 51.—Owen Gallagher, æt. 27. Fell from a height striking on his knees, Jan. 8, 1868, and breaking the right patella (comminuted.)

He was admitted to First Surg. Div., Bellevue Hospital, Jan. 20th. On the 22d, two weeks after the accident, my inclined plane apparatus was applied. Up to this time, owing to the swelling, etc., no splint had been applied.

Feb. 1st.—My service terminated, the limb being still in the apparatus.

United by ligament half an inch long.

COMMINUTED FRACTURE.—DIRECT FORCE.—SUPPOSED BONY UNION.

CASE 52.—Charles Jones, æt. 5. Fell on his left knee, Jan. 31, 1848, breaking off a small fragment from the upper and inner margin of the patella. When the leg was flexed it became tilted forwards, and projected sharply under the skin ; but when the leg was straight, it resumed its natural position in contact with the body of the patella.

Dr. Austin Flint and myself being in attendance, we applied a straight posterior splint, and six months after no traces of the injury remained.

CASE 53.—Wm. P., æt. 25. Fell Dec. 27, 1853, breaking his left thigh and patella. The thigh was broken in its middle third. The patella was broken transversely in its middle, and vertically near its inner margin. Drs. E. and D., were in attendance until the fifth day, when I was added to the consultation. We laid the limb upon a single inclined plane, securing the fragments of the patella in apposition as near as possible with adhesive strips and a roller. The patella had united on the fifty-eighth day.

Five months after the fracture occurred, I found the main fragments separated half an inch ; the bond of union feeling firm like bone. The small lateral fragments had not united, and it was movable. He had but little motion at the knee-joint, but was able to walk and to pursue his occupation as a carpenter. The femur had united with a shortening of half an inch.

FRACTURE OF BOTH PATELLÆ, AT DIFFERENT TIMES, FROM DIRECT FORCE.—FIBROUS UNION.—SUBSEQUENT RUPTURE OF BOTH LIGA-MENTS, AND NO UNION.

CASES 54 and 55.—Jeremiah Murphy, of No. 3 Bridge Street, New York, æt. 56, broke his *left* patella transversely, below the middle, by a fall upon the knee. A surgeon of this city was called and applied bandages. He was four or five weeks in bed, and then went out, using a cane. Fragments were then found to be separated. Aug. 30, 1879, 17 years after the accident, I found the fragments separated 3½ inches when the leg was straight, and 4¾ when it is flexed. Fragments of normal size. No ligament between fragments; but along their outer and inner margins the tendinous fibres of the quadriceps are prominent, and especially on the outer side. He cannot extend the leg by muscular action when sitting, but he can flex it to an acute angle with the thigh. Standing, he can flex and extend it perfectly. In extending he turns the foot out, in order to bring into action the outer portion of the quadriceps. He has always, since the first accident, been some lame with the leg, but could walk several miles, and carry loads without a cane.

May 25*th*, 1879, he slipped and fell, striking upon the *right* knee and breaking the *right* patella transversely about its middle. Dr. S. called : very much swollen. June 1, Dr. S. applied adhesive strips over and about the patella, then a plaster-of-Paris bandage from the hollow of the foot to above the knee. Fragments were separated an inch or more. Began to walk. A few days later the leg suddenly gave way and he fell back. The skin became discolored, and it swelled very much.

Fragments now separated 1¾ inches, when the limb is straight, and 3 inches when it is flexed. He walks slowly without a cane ; but is in constant fear of falling. I advise him to submit to a second trial to obtain a more satisfactory result in the case of the right leg.

SECOND PAPER.

The first paper (55 cases) was devoted to those cases only which had come under my own observation; and it was my intention now to publish such Bellevue Hospital cases as have not been seen by me, and for the correctness of which the hospital records are mainly or wholly responsible. I find, however, that some of them were seen by me, and notes were taken, by which in part these reports will be governed. Of a few other hospital cases my private notes supply records, while no account of them has been found in the hospital books. Possibly in the search they have been overlooked.

Three or four have been added which were at the time of treatment more or less under my observation in the Reception Hospitals, which were at one time auxiliary to Bellevue. The notes were taken by me while I occupied the position of Surgeon-in-chief of these Hospitals. Of course they do not comprise all of the cases treated in these hospitals.

Hereafter I shall not attempt to present the cases in a classified order, having found this exceedingly difficult to do in a manner to be absolutely correct, or profitable to the reader.

SIMPLE TRANSVERE FRACTURE, FROM DIRECT FORCE—FIBROUS UNION OF ½ INCH—RUPTURE AND FIBROUS UNION OF 1 INCH —RUPTURE AND NO UNION. (Seen by the writer).

CASE 56.—John Smith, laborer, æt., 25, slipped on an icy sidewalk, Jan. 10, 1871, striking the right knee and breaking the patella transversely at the lower end of upper fourth. Dr. M., of this city, applied a plaster-of-Paris splint on the third day. Kept in bed three or four weeks and then walked about a little. Removed at end of six weeks. Found fragments united with a separation of about half an inch, with but little motion in the joint. He was told to go to work, having an elastic kneecap upon the knee and leg. One week later his foot twisted a little under him; he felt a sharp pain in the knee and found the fragments much separated. A good deal of swelling ensued. Four days later Dr. B. put on a posterior leather splint, and this was kept on eight weeks, during most of which time he was in bed. Fragments were then found united, with a separation of half an inch or more. He was then permitted to go out, with the posterior splint still applied.

Four weeks later, in descending a flight of steps, while bending the knee slightly, the fragments parted again. Dr. S. was now called, and for three months Drs. S. and V. tried to make the fragments unite, but could not, the patient being kept in bed, and the parts supported with adhesive straps.

I examined Mr. Smith, Oct. 1, 1879. The fragments are separated 3½ inches, and he can flex the joint only 10°: cannot extend it. There is no bond of union. The fragments are not enlarged. The upper fragment is very small and fixed. The lower is tilted, so that the separation is greater on the inside than outer. He can only extend his leg by turning it in very much, when the vastus externus, which is attached to the lower fragment alone, lifts the leg. In ascending steps he drags the lame leg after the other, yet he walks very well on a level surface. Muscles of thigh are wasted. Has worn a knee-cap for 4 or 5 years, and says he cannot walk well without it.

SIMPLE TRANSVERSE FRACTURE AT THE MIDDLE, FROM DIRECT FORCE—FIBROUS UNION, OF ½ INCH.   (Seen by the writer.)

CASE 57.—Wm. Marr, æt. 43. Oct. 19, 1875, fell and struck upon his left knee, his knee striking upon a bar of iron.

Oct. 21.—He was admitted to Bellevue, 2d Surg. Div., Dr. Markoe's service. The patella was broken transversely at its middle, and the fragments were separated one inch. The knee was swollen. A pasteboard, posterior splint was applied, and secured by a roller.

Oct. 28.—Swelling has subsided. Considerable ecchymosis. Case presented to the class in the amphitheatre by Dr. Markoe.

Oct. 29.—10th day. Two crescentic pieces of wood were placed above and below the fragments, adhesive strips were applied, and by some contrivance the crescentic blocks were rendered adjustable.

Oct. 31.—Apparatus painful and not satisfactory, and removed.

Nov. 1.—Circular adhesive strips applied, and these were approximated by counter bands of cotton roller, bringing the fragments into apposition. The limb was supported by a posterior wooden splint.

Nov. 5.—Has an attack of pleuritis.

Nov. 19.—Fragments in "good position."

Nov. 26.—38th day. A plaster-of-Paris splint applied, and patient allowed to go about on crutches.

Dec. 16.—58th day. Plaster-of-Paris splint removed. Fragments in good apposition and united firmly. Can bend the knee a little, and can walk by the exercise of caution. An elastic knee-cap applied.

Jan. 7, 1876.—90th day. Can walk quite well on a horizontal surface by the aid of a cane. Discharged.

I saw the man Oct. 2, 1879, nearly four years after the accident. Wore elastic knee-cap about three months. Has now perfect use of limb. Fragments separated half an inch, and the bond of union feels like bone, but the fragments can be moved slightly upon each other, showing that it is fibrous.

SIMPLE TRANSVERSE FRACTURE FROM DIRECT FORCE.—LIGAMENTOUS
UNION OF ¾ INCH.

CASE 58.—Maria Mossopp, æt. 25, broke the patella transversely by a fall upon a brick, May 26, 1866. Admitted to Bellevue, on the following day. The fragments were separated one inch and three-quarters.

May 29.—My inclined plane apparatus was applied, and, in

addition, long oblique straps, enclosing the thigh, and secured by cords to the foot piece, in order to antagonize the quadriceps.

June 1.—The long adhesive straps were found loose, and were removed on account of vesications caused by them above the patella.

July 9.--Posterior splint and knee-cap substituted, and patient allowed to get out of bed.

Sept. 15--Discharged (nearly four months from time of accident). Ligamentous union of three-quarters of an inch.

SIMPLE TRANSVERSE FRACTURE FROM DIRECT BLOW —MALGAIGNE'S HOOKS—FIBROUS UNION (?) OF ¼ INCH.

CASE 59.—Maria Masson, æt. 27. Had her left patella broken transversely from direct violence, Aug. 20, 1867. Admitted on same day to 1st Surg. Div., Bellevue. On examination, the fragments were found separated three-quarters of an inch, and the parts much swollen.

The limb was placed upon an inclined plane, without dressings, and evaporating lotion applied.

Aug. 31.—Eleventh day. Adhesive strips were applied to secure apposition of fragments, the limb still resting upon the inclined plane.

Sept. 3.—Fourteenth day. Malgaigne's hooks were applied (see Fig. 214, p. 471, of the 5th ed. of my work on Fractures and Dislocations.) Instead, however, of making the points penetrate the skin and bone, as practiced by Malgaigne, a small piece of leather was placed above and below, on the edges of the fragments, and over these several layers of adhesive plaster. The hooks were then applied. The points caused some pain, and a small piece of tin was laid over the leather and plaster, and the hooks reapplied.

Oct. 8.—The hooks were removed, and then reapplied.

Oct. 26. Sixty-seven days after the injury, and fifty-three after the hooks were applied, apparatus removed finally. The joint was quite stiff, and the fragments separated one-quarter of an inch. We presume that from the record we may infer that the bond of union was ligamentous, yet this is not stated. She was discharged Nov. 26.

(There is much reason to suppose that this case was in the same person as Case 58, and that it was a *rupture* or *re-fracture.*)

SIMPLE TRANSVERSE FRACTURE.

CASE 60.—Bridget Callahan, æt. 80, fell about thirteen feet, Jan. 7, 1871, breaking the right patella. Admitted to Bellevue on the same day. Second Surg. Div. Her limb was laid upon an inclined plane, and the fragments secured with figure of-8 bandage.

Subsequently the limb was dressed with a plaster-of-Paris bandage, extending from the ankle to the hip, with an opening above the knee. The fragments being secured with adhesive strips laid obliquely, and a roller.

Jan. 27. — "Fragments in close apposition." (There are no farther notes of this case.)

COMMINUTED FRACTURE, COMPLICATED WITH OTHER INJURIES—DIED OF SHOCK ON 4TH DAY.

CASE 61.—George Christ, æt. 21, was run over by a street car Sept. 1, 1869, and was admitted on the same day to the 2d Surg. Div.; Dr. A. Mott's service ; having sustained a compound fracture of the left femur, and a comminuted fracture of the left patella.

He died of shock on the fourth day.

SIMPLE TRANSVERSE FRACTURE — DISCHARGED "CURED" IN 61 DAYS.

CASE 62.—Julia Carr, æt. 42, fell upon her knee, striking the edge of a step, Feb. 11, 1877 ; on same day admitted to 3d Surg. Div. Bellevue.

Fracture transverse, and separation one-half inch. Buck's extension was applied, with a posterior splint. The fragments being secured with a many tailed bandage.

April 13.—Sixty-one days—discharged "cured." (Here the record closes.)

TRANSVERSE FRACTURE FROM DIRECT FORCE—FIBROUS UNION OF ½ INCH. (Not found in Hospital Record, but seen by myself.)

CASE 63.—Wm. Smith, æt. 25, fell upon his right knee Dec. 26,

1875, and on the same day was admitted to Bellevue, ward 11 Five days later a plaster-of-Paris splint was applied by one of the house surgeons. This was removed at the end of six weeks and reapplied. It was removed finally about the middle of March, having been on the limb about ten weeks. The fragments were separated half an inch, with a fibrous bond of union. Could move the joint slightly.

SIMPLE TRANSVERSE FRACTURE FROM MUSCULAR ACTION.—NO BOND OF UNION.—SEPARATION OF 3¼ INCHES. (seen by the writer in 1879.)

CASE 64.—John Hennesy, æt. 27, slipped May 7th, 1872, in descending a flight of steps, and doubled his left leg under him sharply. He did not feel any thing give way, but he found he could only walk with help. A surgeon of this city was called, who put on a straight splint, the knee being much swollen. About the third day a plaster-of-Paris splint was applied, which was kept on about two weeks. After this the posterior splint was reapplied. He used a cane nine months, and bandaged the leg for a year.

I saw this man, through the courtesy of Dr. L. D. Buckley, Sept. 29, 1879, more than seven years after the accident. The fracture was transverse, below the middle. The upper fragment is considerably hypertrophied. When the limb is straight the fragments separate 2½ inches, and when flexed, 3¼ inches. There is no evidence of any bond of union between the fragments. He can flex the leg perfectly but cannot, by the muscles alone, extend it completely. He walks very well on a level surface, but is very liable to fall. In ascending steps he drags the left leg after him. It is occasionally painful, and if he stands much the joint becomes filled with fluid.

SIMPLE TRANSVERSE FRACTURE FROM MUSCULAR ACTION.—FIBROUS UNION OF ⅓ INCH.

CASE 65.—Nelly Strong, æt. 23, admitted to 4th Surg. Div. Bellevue, Feb. 21, 1876, having just broken her left patella transversely below its middle. She stated that she slipped in descending a flight of steps and twisted her ankle, and that attempting to support her self the patella broke. (Her nose had been partly destroyed by "lupus" and a tolerably successful operation had been made for its restoration, from the upper lip.)

On admission the knee was greatly swollen. The limb was laid upon a straight splint and evaporating lotions applied. On the 24th the swelling had begun to subside, and the fragments were found separated ¼ inch.

Feb. 29.—Adhesive strips applied in the form of the "lock strap," but it would not bring the fragments together.

March 6.—(2 weeks) Plaster-of-Paris splint applied, but it caused so much pain that it had to be removed, and on the following day a posterior leather splint was applied, with adhesive strips to support the fragments.

March 29.—Splint removed and re-applied, after giving to the joint slight motion.

April 4.—Fragments separated ⅓ inch. Daily passive motion.

April 26—Splint still on leg. Discharged "cured." We may presume that a fibrous union occurred, as the exact amount of separation is given.

SIMPLE TRANSVERSE FRACTURE FROM MUSCULAR ACTION ; FOLLOWING A SLIGHT INJURY—FIBROUS UNION OF ½ INCH.

CASE 66.—Thomas Shielab, æt. 42, admitted Jan. 10, 1878, to Bellevue Hospital, 2d Surg. Div. He states that two months before he hit his left knee against a ladder, causing some pain, but he continued to perform his duties as a fireman. This morning, standing at the corner of the street, he turned suddenly and fell upon his lame knee, and could not rise. On admission there was considerable swelling. Fracture of left patella; transverse, at upper end of lower ⅓. A posterior splint was applied and an evaporating lotion.

Jan. 21.—Swelling gone ; bandage applied over splint and knee to support fragments.

Jan. 27.—Bandage has slipped; reapplied; no pain and doing well.

Feb. 1 (22d day).—Plaster-of-Paris splint applied and kept on one month ; then passive motion employed.

April 6, (3 months).—Discharged. Firm fibrous union, fragments being separated ½ inch; motion one·third normal.

SIMPLE TRANSVERSE FRACTURE FROM MUSCULAR ACTION— FIBROUS UNION ¾ INCH—OPPOSITE PATELLA BROKEN IN SAME MANNER, FROM MUSCULAR ACTION, NEARLY SIXTEEN MONTHS LATER.— FIBROUS UNION ¾ INCH. (Seen by the writer in 1879.)

CASES 67–8.—Margaret Woods, 240 E. 75th St., æt. 25, in descending a flight of steps Sept. 14, 1877, caught her foot and fell, breaking the right patella transversely below its middle from muscular action. She felt it break. Sept. 15 removed to Bellevue, 4th Surg. Div., Dr. E. Mason's service. The fragments were found separated ⅝ inch. A posterior splint was applied with a bandage.

Oct. 2.—Dr. A. Mott's apparatus substituted. This caused her considerable pain. Oct. 8th it was removed and adhesive plasters were applied to reduce fragments, and over this a plaster-of-Paris splint. (Hospital record here terminates.)

When she consulted me Sept., 1879, she informed me that the plaster splint was kept on six weeks. She was discharged Dec. 26th, 1877. Some time later she laid aside her crutches.

Jan. 1, 1879.—In descending a flight of steps her foot turned, and in attempting to support herself she broke the left patella in the same manner and at the same point as the right. She did not fall. She was taken to Roosevelt Hospital, service of Dr. Sands. A simple bandage was applied ·for two weeks, and then a silicate-of-soda splint was applied, which remained on six weeks. April 9th she left the hospital on crutches.

Sept. 26, 1879.—More than two years after the first accident I found both patellæ united with ligaments of about ¾ of an inch in length. Some grating under the fragments. She could walk without a cane on a level surface ; could flex and extend both legs perfectly, but could not go up and down stairs ; considerable pain in knees ; had not been out of the house for a long time.

I advised use of the limbs out of doors, and electricity.

SIMPLE TRANSVERSE FRACTURE FROM MUSCULAR ACTION—NO TREATMENT FOR SIX WEEKS.—FIBROUS UNION OF ⅜ INCH.

CASE 69.—Catherine Connor, æt. 20, in jumping from a carriage, broke the right patella transversely. Muscular action. She says nothing was done for the fracture, but that she remained in bed six weeks, or up to the time of admission to Bellevue.

Admitted to First Surgical. Division, April 6, 1866. Fragments separated two inches. The limb was laid upon an inclined plane, and adhesive strips applied longitudinally from above and below over the patella, and so interlocked as to draw the fragments together. April 16, dressings reapplied.

May 12.—Dressings finally removed. Fragments united by a ligament of three-eighths-of-an-inch (36 days after apparatus was applied, and about 11 weeks after the fracture was received.)

May 19.—Walking on crutches.

Aug. 16.—Discharged—nearly five mouths after the injury was received. Could not then walk without crutches.

SIMPLE TRANSVERSE FRACTURE, PROBABLY FROM MUSCULAR AC-TION.—PLASTER–OF–PARIS AND OTHER DRESSINGS—FIBROUS UNION OF ¼ INCH.

(Seen by the writer.)

CASE 70.—Wm. Masterson, æt. 30, caught his foot and fell when three steps from the bottom of a flight of steps, not falling heavily upon the floor, when he felt something give way in his knee. He was admitted on the same day, Dec. 15, 1878, to Bellevue, 2d Surg. Div., and was found to have a transverse fracture of the left patella. There was slight effusion into the joint. A posterior splint was applied, and the fragments were supported by a bandage. Ice-bags applied to knee.

Dec. 19.—Ice-bags discontinued and " wooden fingers" appled to support the fragments.

Dec. 20.—Not able to bear the pain caused by the "wooden fingers." Straps were placed under them and over the patella.

Dec. 31.—Straps have loosened. Replaced.

Jan. 6.—Form and position of straps changed, and their ends tacked to the posterior splint, and over this a roller bandage.

Jan. 7.—Complains of pain; roller bandage too tight ; removed ; the other bands continued ; foot raised.

Jan. 17.—Fibrous union. Fragments separated ¼ inch. Plaster-of-Paris splint applied (33rd day), foot swelled and it was cut open next day.

Dec. 18.—Sitting up.

Discharged in February.

I examined Mr. Masterson Oct. 1, 1879. Found the fragments united by a ligament of half-an-inch. No hypertrophy. · Flexes and extends leg perfectly. Drags the leg in going up stairs. Hurts in descending. Walks well on a level surface.

Mr. M. says that when the splint was removed the joint was quite stiff. Wore a bandage and knee-cap occasionally since, but not lately. Never used any force to overcome the anchylosis. Obtained free motion in about two months, using passive motion.

SIMPLE TRANSVERSE FRACTURE, FROM MUSCULAR ACTION—FIBROUS UNION, ½ INCH.   (Seen by the writer.)

CASE 71.—Henry Scombs, æt., 49, weighing 200 lbs., was admitted to Bellevue, 2d Surg. Div., Nov. 6, 1878. On the same day he tripped and fell down a flight of steps, but did not strike his knee. He was found to have a transverse fracture of the right patella below its middle. The fragments separated ¾ inch. Some swelling and effusion into the joint, ecchymosis ; complete loss of power to extend limb, but not much pain. Splint and adhesive strips were applied, but the fragments were not brought into contact.

Nov. 11.—Effusion continues; no pain ; adhesive plasters removed, and with the fingers fragments easily brought together ;

carved pieces of wood to represent fingers—were placed above and below and secured with adhesive strips, bringing the fragments into apposition ; but he was unable to bear the pain they caused, and they were removed the same day; adhesive strips alone were again employed; icebags applied.

Nov. 15.—Ice suspended ; "wooden fingers" again tried, but the pain again compelled their removal, and the substitution of adhesive strips.

Nov. 19.—Adhesive strips removed ; plaster-of-Paris bandage applied. On the same day the record says: "No pain or trouble;" (probably because there was no farther attempt to bring the fragments together.—H.)

Feb. 22.—Discharged.

I saw this patient Sept. 29, 1879, nearly 11 months after the accident. He says the plaster-of-Paris was on the limb 11 weeks, and that when it was removed his knee was quite stiff. He used crutches for a time.

When examined by me the fragments were found united by a ligament half an inch in length and so firm that it felt like bone ; but there was a marked depression between the fragments, and the fragments could be moved separately, but the motion was very slight. The fragments were somewhat hypertrophied. All the motions of the joint were completely restored, and even in ascending stairs he used both legs alike, but in descending a slight halt was noticeable.

COMMINUTED FRACTURE, FROM DIRECT FORCE—FIBROUS UNION.

CASE 72.—Frank O'Baine, æt. 32. Fell 3 or 4 steps, striking on left patella, June 5th, 1879, and 3 or 4 hours later was admitted to Bellevue—1st, Surg. Div. There was already great swelling over the front and sides of the knee, with marked ecchymosis, especially in front of the patella. Pain and crepitus. The fracture was transverse, the lower fragment being broken again vertically. The upper fragment was separated 1 inch, and the lower fragments were separated from each other ½ an inch. Icebags applied. June 13th, swelling diminished. Ice discontinued.

June 16.—The fragments were supported with India-rubber adhesive plaster and roller. The whole limb being enclosed in a plaster-of-Paris splint reinforced by pasteboard posteriorly, and having a window over the joint.

July 7.—Removed the plaster splint. Fragments appear to be united. Movable upon each other. A posterior pasteboard splint applied.

July 11.—Posterior splint removed.

July 18.—Went out on pass and did not return.

SIMPLE OBLIQUE FRACTURE.

CASE 73.—E. M. Freligh, æt. 45. Jan. 3, 1876, fell down a flight of door steps, striking upon his forehead, and upon his knee slightly flexed. He was unable to rise. Admitted to Bellevue, 2d. Surg. Div., on same day.

The joint was so much swollen that the patella could not be felt. Lead and opium wash.

Jan. 7.—4th day—first recognized an oblique fracture. A posterior splint was applied, with circular and oblique turns of a roller, leaving the front of the knee exposed, so as to apply lead and opium wash.

Jan. 19.—16th day—swelling nearly gone. A posterior splint was applied, and over this, crossing the front of the thigh just above the patella, a circular band of India rubber tubing. On each side of the leg long adhesive strips were passed under the tubing and brought down the sides of the leg and under the hollow of the foot. He complained at once that the apparatus was painful, and on the following day it became necessary to loosen it (here the record closes.)

SIMPLE TRANSVERSE FRACTURE—FIG-OF-8, AND PLASTER.—ULCERATIONS AND SLOUGH. "CURED."

CASE 74.—John Grey, æt. 41. Admitted May 19, 1875, to 3d Surg. Div., Bellevue, having just received injuries from a policeman's club.

There was found among other injuries a transverse fracture of the patella, caused by a blow from the club, the fragments being separated ½ an inch. He was intoxicated.

A posterior splint was applied and the fragments supported by a figure-of-8 bandage.

May 26.—A figure-of-8 bandage was laid around the limb, with pads above and below the knee, to draw the fragments together, and then a plaster-of-Paris splint was applied from the ankle to the upper third of the thigh. A window being cut over the patella. At first this was left open, but when the swelling subsided a roller was carried over this part.

June 8.—13 days after its application the plaster was removed. The figure-of-8 had caused ulceration above and below the knee. The plaster and other retentive dressings omitted.

June 21.—" Sloughs almost healed," and plaster-of-Paris splint again applied.

July 16.—" Discharged cured."

SIMPLE TRANSVERSE FRACTURE—DIRECT BLOW—FIBROUS UNION—
REFRACTURE FROM MUSCULAR ACTION AFTER THREE MONTHS
—RESULT UNKNOWN.

CASE 75.—Wm. Baker, æt. 36, fell April 11, 1877, striking his right knee upon a curb stone, causing a transverse fracture. He was sent to Long Island College Hospital, where he remained nearly three months and was then discharged cured.

On the day of his discharge, July 8th, he was walking quickly when he felt his knee give way suddenly, and was taken to Bellevue, 4th Surg. Div. There was not much swelling or tenderness. A temporary dressing was applied, and on the 14th Dr. Mott's apparatus was substituted. Pads made of cork and covered with chamois, beveled on the under surface, crescentic in shape, were placed above and below the fragments. These were held in place by two pieces of webbing, each six inches wide, and which encircled the limb; they were then made to approach each other by counter strips of webbing, stitched to one of the circular straps and buckled to the other. The fragments were coapted.

Aug. 1.—The above dressing was removed, having been on two weeks. "Upper crescent has slipped over the upper fragment. There is about ⅜ of an inch separation between the fragments."

Aug. 8.—A figure-of-8 bandage applied, over a posterior splint. (No further record of the case.)

SIMPLE TRANSVERSE FRACTURE—FIBROUS UNION, ½ INCH.

CASE 76.—Catharine Connoly, admitted to Bellevue, 4th Surg. Div., March 27, 1876. Intemperate.

Six weeks before, she fell in climbing a fence and broke her left patella transversely, at the middle.

She was taken to Charity Hospital, where a posterior splint and bandage were applied.

On admission to Bellevue the fragments were separated ½ inch. The same treatment was continued.

July 2.—After more than three months discharged "cured."

SIMPLE TRANSVERSE FRACTURE FROM DIRECT FORCE —UNION BY LIGAMENT OF ¾ INCH.

CASE 77.—Mary Seymour, æt. 40, broke right patella transversely April 30, 1866; caused by a fall down a flight of stairs, striking upon the knee.

May 1.—Admitted to Bellevue, 1st Surg. Div. There was extensive ecchymosis and swelling, with great pain. The knee-joint was suffering from acute synovitis and was much distended. Owing to these circumstances the fracture was not recognized until the second day after admission, but the limb was kept extended and at rest. The fragments were then found separated two inches.

May 10.—The same apparatus was employed as in the case of Catharine Connor, namely, the inclined plane and longitudinal adhesive strips.

May 12.—Removed and reapplied.

May 15.—Removed and reapplied.

June 12.—Adhesive strips removed ; inclined plane continued.

July. 30.—An abscess opened upon back of thigh just below trochanter major. On the same day she was discharged, the fragments having united with a ligament of ¾ of an inch.

Mary died in 1874, and up to a short time before death was able to work, only complaining of her knee in damp weather.

SIMPLE FRACTURE—LIGAMENTOUS UNION OF ¾ INCH.

CASE 78.—Robert Wood, æt. 40, fell March 2, 1866, breaking the patella. He was admitted to 2d Surg. Div., Bellevue, March 7th. On the 8th Dr. Mott's apparatus was applied and the limb kept upon an inclined plane.

March 25.—Apparatus removed ; inclined plane continued.

March 28.—Pillows substituted for the inclined plane. Ligamentous union of ¾ of an inch—26 days after the fracture.

April 7.—Posterior splint applied and patient allowed to go about on crutches. On the following day discharged.

SIMPLE TRANSVERSE FRACTURE FROM DIRECT FORCE. UNION BY LIGAMENT OF ¼ INCH. RUPTURED THIRTY-EIGHT DAYS AFTER THE FIRST ACCIDENT. UNITED AGAIN BY LIGAMENT OF ½ INCH.

CASE 79.—Henry Sloan, æt. 30. Received a blow from a club upon his knee, causing a transverse fracture at its middle. He was admitted on the same day, Feb. 27, 1866, to Second Surgical Division of Bellevue Hospital. The fragments were separated half an inch.

Feb. 28.—My inclined plane apparatus applied. Next day it was found loose and was readjusted; with the addition of long adhesive strips laid obliquely along the thigh, and made fast to the foot-board of the apparatus by two lateral cords; the object being to act upon and diminish the contractile power of the quadriceps muscles.

March 23.—Twenty-three days. The dressings were removed, and the fragments were found united by a ligament one-quarter of an inch in length. He was directed to remain in bed without apparatus.

April 6.—Had been walking (fourteen days after the dressings were removed and thirty-eight after the fracture) and fell, rupturing the ligament.   My apparatus and the adhesive strips again applied, as before.

May 5.—One month after last fracture, apparatus removed.   A posterior splint and knee-cap substituted.   Ligamentous union of half an inch.

June 12.—Discharged.

SIMPLE TRANSVERSE FRACTURE—ALMOST NO TREATMENT—LIGA-
MENTOUS UNION—RUPTURE OF LIGAMENT THREE MONTHS AFTER
FIRST ACCIDENT—LIGAMENTOUS UNION OF ¾ INCH.

CASE 80.—Ed. Cavanaugh, æt. 24, broke his patella transversely Dec. 27, 1865.   He says he had no other treatment than that he remained in bed with a bandage on his leg for a time, and then walked about with a cane.

March 25, three months after the first accident, as he was descending a flight of stairs, his leg turned under him, and he ruptured the ligament.   He was admitted to Bellevue on the same day—2d Surgical Division.

March 26.—My inclined plane apparatus was applied.

April 16.—Twenty-two days after the re-fracture.   There was said to be ligamentous union.

April 24.—Thirty days after the refracture, the apparatus was removed and a posterior leather splint substituted, and he was permitted to use crutches.

May 4.—He was discharged, with a ligamentous bond three-fourths of an inch in length.

COMMINUTED FRACTURE FROM DIRECT FORCE—PLASTER-OF-PARIS
SPLINT—ABSCESS—RESULT UNKNOWN.

CASE 81.—Michael Griffin, æt. 48.   Fell on edge of curbstone, Jan. 26, 1871.   An attempt to extend his leg caused great pain.

Admitted to Bellevue, 3d Surg. Div., Jan. 27th.   The patella was found broken into three pieces, first transversely, and the lower fragment vertically.   There was a good deal of swelling and ecchymosis.   Ordered rest and evaporating lotion.

Jan. 31.—Fourth day.   The swelling having subsided, a plaster-of

Paris splint was applied from just above the ankle to the perineum. Where it enclosed the knee, compresses were first laid above and below the knee, and one long one upon the front of the knee, and then the plaster bandages were made to cross the knee in the form of a figure-of-8. The limb, thus enclosed, was laid upon a single inclined plane.

Feb. 3.—Has complained of pain, and the inclined plane was removed, and he was ordered to get up.

Feb. 6.—Sharp pain, with tenderness over the trochanter—superficial—which proved to be an enlargement of the bursa over the trochanter. (Probably due to the chafing of the top of the splint.—F. H. H.) Tinct. of iodine was applied! (Here the record terminates).

SIMPLE TRANSVERSE FRACTURE FROM MUSCULAR ACTION—FIBROUS UNION—RUPTURE OF BOND OF UNION FROM MUSCULAR ACTION AFTER SEVEN WEEKS—FIBROUS UNION AGAIN OF $\frac{1}{4}$ INCH.

CASE 82.—James Lyon, æt. 35, was admitted to Bellevue Hospital, 1st Surg. Div., March 1, 1878. He stated that seven weeks before he had been thrown down, twisting his leg, and that he felt his knee give way. The limb was dressed at a dispensary, and he was laid up ten days.

Feb. 26, these dressings were removed.

Feb. 28, while walking, he felt his knee suddenly give way, and on the following day he was brought to Bellevue.

There was found to be a transverse fracture of the patella below its middle, and crepitus was present. The knee could be partly flexed. An adhesive plaster "lock-strap" was applied, and a plaster-of-Paris splint from the toes to the middle of the thigh.

March 4.—Plaster splint removed and reapplied.

March 25.—Removed and reapplied.

April 9.—Removed: passive motion employed, and the same splint reapplied with dry rollers. Fragments separated $\frac{1}{4}$ inch.

April 23.—Plaster splint removed and leather splint substituted. Movements of joint limited. Went out on pass and did not return.

SIMPLE TRANSVERSE FRACTURE FROM DIRECT BLOW.—RESULT UN-
KNOWN.

CASE 83.—James McCarty, æt. 30, admitted to Bellevue, 4th
Surg. Div., Aug. 6th, 1878, the accident having happened on the
same day. He had fracture of the patella, transverse, a little below
its middle, caused by a direct blow. There was only slight separation of the fragments. The knee was swollen.

Aug 7.—"Lock strap" applied and a posterior splint, the whole
being secured with a silicate of soda bandage.

Aug. 11.—Apparatus removed and re-applied.

Aug. 14.—Again removed and reapplied, and the fragments supported by oblique and circular turns of rollers about the knee.

Sept. 2.—Dressings removed and plaster-of-Paris splint applied.
On the 3d of Sept. he was sitting up. (No further record of the
case.)

SIMPLE TRANSVERSE FRACTURE—DIRECT FORCE—BOND OF UNION
½ INCH.

CASE. 84.—George H. Briggs, æt. 35, fell upon his left knee Dec.
13, 1873, breaking the patella transversely. When he got up he
found he was unable to extend the leg, and he felt a pain over the patella. Admitted Dec. 14, to 2d Surg. Div. Fragments separated
¾ inch. A posterior splint was applied, and the limb treated with
lead and opium wash.

Dec. 23.—Swelling reduced. Adhesive strips were applied to
keep the fragments in position, and a plaster-of-Paris bandage applied from the ankle to the middle of the thigh. Jan. 27th, 1874. Directed to "remove splint daily" (probably a back splint, which had
been substituted for the plaster-of-Paris.)

Feb. 15.—Discharged, with a bond of union of ½ an inch in
length.

SIMPLE TRANSVERSE FRACTURE, FROM MUSCULAR ACTION—RESULT
NOT RECORDED. (Probably same patient as preceding, but the
fracture was in the opposite leg.)

CASE 85.—George H. Briggs, æt. 35, slipped upon an orange peel and trying to save himself felt the right patella "snap." Admitted March 15, 1874, the day of the accident, to the 2d Surg. Div., ward 7. Fragments separated ½ inch. Considerable swelling.

A temporary posterior splint was secured to the limb, with a figure-of-8 bandage, and lead and opium wash applied.

March 21.—Sixth day, small pads were laid above and below the fragments and over these adhesive strips, from above and below, reinforced by broad bands, so as to keep the fragments together. Over this a plaster-of-Paris bandage.

· Here the record of the case terminates.

SIMPLE TRANSVERSE FRACTURE FROM DIRECT BLOW—RESULT NOT RECORDED.

CASE 86.—George A. Bell, æt. 26 ; residence unknown. By a fall upon his knee broke the patella and was admitted to the 2d Surg. Div., June 6, 1873.

Fracture transverse at junction of upper and middle thirds. Considerable swelling of joint. Lead and opium wash.

June 18.—Swelling nearly gone. Leg snugly bandaged. Fragments separated ½ inch. (No farther record of this case.)

SIMPLE FRACTURE—"DRESSINGS" ENDANGER THE VITALITY OF THE LIMB—RESULT NOT RECORDED.

CASE 87.—Rudolph King, residence unknown, fell July 27th, 1875, from a third story, breaking his left patella and the inferior maxilla. He was admitted to 2d Surg. Div., Bellevue on the same day. When admitted he was unconscious.

Aug. 1.—Fifth day, "a dressing is to-day applied for fractured patella," (probably plaster-of-Paris.)

Aug. 3.—Dressings removed, "as foot looks very bad." Foot was enveloped in cotton wadding and elevated.

Aug. 5.—Hot water and alcohol applied, and removed as often as it became cool.

Aug. 10.—"Circulation returning." Fragments separated ½ inch. (This closes the record.)

SIMPLE TRANSVERSE FRACTURE FROM DIRECT BLOW, RESULT NOT KNOWN.

Case 88.—Charles Henry, residence unknown, æt 21. Fell on his left knee, March 26, 1871, breaking the patella transversely. Admitted on same day to 2d Surg. Div. The fracture was across the middle, and the fragments were separated half an inch. Rest alone was enjoined.

March 27.—Plaster-of-Paris dressing applied from the ankle to the groin. (Here the record closes).

SIMPLE TRANSVERSE FRACTURE—WALKED TEN DAYS—NOT REC-OGNIZED BY THE FIRST SURGEON—FIBROUS UNION.

Case 89.—Jerry Burke, 27 Rose st., æt. 24. Slipped and fell on the deck of a ship Sept. 11, 1877. Says he was sent to the Jersey City Hospital, and that the surgeon said he had only sprained his leg, and they would not admit him. He walked about till the 21st—ten days—and then went to Chambers Street Hospital, where the fracture was recognized, and he was sent the same day, to Bellevue Hospital, 3d Surg. Div.

Found to have a transverse fracture of the left patella. The limb was secured to an inclined plane with a roller, and fragments held by adhesive strips, "locked."

Oct. 2.—"Lock-strap" removed and two elastic bandages substituted, one passing from above and across the patella obliquely, and the other from below obliquely, and both made fast with buckles to the inclined plane.

Nov. 1.—Above removed and "lock-strap" substituted, and a light plaster-of-Paris splint applied over all.

Nov. 2.—Removed plaster splint. (Kept on only one day).

Nov. 23.—Fibrous union—seventy-four days. Passive motion.

Dec. 6.—Walks about.

Jan. 7.—Four months. Discharged "cured."

COMPOUND, COMMINUTED "STELLATED" FRACTURE FROM DIRECT
FORCE—FIBROUS UNION AND REFRACTURE—SEPARATION OF TWO
INCHES—THE QUESTION OF FINAL UNION NOT DETERMINED.

CASE 90.—Pat. Farren, residence unknown, æt. 66, June 11th,
1868. A mass of iron rolled upon him, throwing him down, and
forcing his left knee against the iron. Admitted to Bellevue Hospital,
3d Surg. Div., on the same day. The fracture was stellated. There
was a wound one and a half inches in length, crossing transversely
the inferior border of the. patella. A finger introduced through this
into the joint disclosed the fact that the joint was filled with blood.
The limb was laid on a straight splint, Buck's extension, with a
weight of five pounds, and cold water dressings were applied.

June 12.—Had a chill.

June 13.—Pulse 104; the weight of extension increased. Quinine
and opium.

June 14.—Less extension. Limb elevated.

June 17.—Ecchymosis in popliteal space. Inclined plane. Ten
pounds extension.

June 23.—Fluctuation in joint. Extension removed.

July 16.—Wounds healed.

July 30.—Fibrous union. Free motion (forty-nine days).

Aug. 25th.—Seventy-five days after the fracture, and twenty-six
after the union was said to be consummated, he was carrying a pail
of water up the steps in the hospital, when he felt a snap in the knee,
and at once lost the power of walking. Admitted to the ward, the
fibrous bond was found broken, and the knee much swollen.

Aug. 29.—Discolored.

Aug. 30.—Swelling less.

Sept. 8.—The joint continuing swollen, a sponge compress was
applied, and Buck's extension, ten pounds.

Sept. 22.—Sponge removed. Swelling gone. Fragments separated two inches.

Sept. 24.—Straps applied and limbs bandaged.

Oct. 3.—Discharged.

SIMPLE TRANSVERSE FRACTURE FROM DIRECT BLOW.   UNITED IN
THREE OR FOUR MONTHS.

CASE 91.—Alexander McKay, adult, residence unknown, Feb. 22, 1875. Slipped and fell on left knee, breaking the patella transversely. Feb. 23, taken to the Park Hospital, where a posterior splint was applied, and on the 26th he was sent to Bellevue Hospital, 3d Surg. Div. On admission the fragments were found separated three-quarters of an inch to one inch. Knee swollen. Lead and opium wash ordered.

March.—Plaster-of-Paris splint applied from the toes to above the knee ; bandages being carried about the knee in the form of a figure-of-8.

May 27.—Ninety-four days from date of injury, and probably more than two months after the plaster splint was applied, it was cut open. Union of fragments said not to be firm.

On the following day, May 28, a new splint of plaster was applied.

June.—Plaster splint cut open, after having been worn about three months. Union firm.

July.—" Discharged."

SIMPLE TRANSVERSE FRACTURE FROM MUSCULAR ACTION—PERHAPS
THE BONE WAS DISEASED—PLASTER-OF-PARIS   DRESSING—RESULT
UNKNOWN.

CASE 92.—Jane Boyle, residence unknown, æt. 29. June 14, 1874, in descending a flight of steps, not rapidly, her right knee suddenly gave way under her, and at the next step she fell, and was unable to rise.

Admitted to Bellevue, 3d Surg. Div., on same day. Her habits were intemperate, and she had had wandering pains in her limbs, and especially in the knee, for some time. Denied having had syphilis ! The fracture was transverse above the middle. The skin was bruised and swollen, and the fragments separated ½ inch. A plaster-of-Paris splint was applied. (No farther record.)

SIMPLE TRANSVERSE FRACTURE FROM DIRECT BLOW.

CASE 93.—Francis Rice, of Long Island City, æt. 43, admitted Jan. 10, 1879, to 3d Surg. Div. On same day, in descending a flight of steps he slipped and struck the outside of his knee against a door. The fracture was transverse; the fragments were separated ¾ inch. Crepitus was easily obtained.

Rubber band was employed to hold the fragments in position.

Jan. 13.—The lock-strap was substituted, and a posterior splint applied. (No farther record.)

COMPOUND, COMPLICATED FRACTURE—SUPPURATION IN KNEE-JOINT—GANGRENE—AMPUTATION ON 34TH DAY—DEATH ON SAME DAY.

CASE 94.—John Ardenbach, æt. 45, fell height of one story, Oct. 15, 1870. Admitted to 2d Surg. Div. same day. Compound fracture of left femur and patella. Limb laid straight, and wound over patella, dressed with lint and collodion. Great amount of discharge from wound over patella.

Oct. 18.—Incision made upon a fluctuating point, but pus not reached. Carbolized oil dressings.

Oct. 24.—Another incision, but no pus.

Oct. 28.—Chills. Quinine, gr. 7, every three hours.

The chills continued to recur at intervals; he was occasionally delirious; the discharge was abundant and fœtid, and on the 13th of Nov. a gangrenous spot was seen below the knee. Meanwhile the quinine had been continued at the rate of gr. 7 every four hours.

Nov. 18.—The gangrene extending and all the symptoms becoming steadily more grave, it was decided to amputate as a last resort. Circular amputation in the lower third of the thigh. Patient did not rally, and died at 8 P. M.

TRANSVERSE AND VERTICAL (COMMINUTED) FRACTURE—RESULT UNKNOWN.

CASE 95.—John M. Vanderveer, 333 E. 61st st., colored, æt. 25, in jumping from a railroad car while in motion broke the right patella, Oct. 9, 1871. On the following day admitted to Bellevue, 2d Surg. Div. The patella was broken transversely in its middle, and the upper fragment was broken in two pieces, vertically.

A plaster-of-Paris dressing was immediately applied, but it was removed on the 6th day—Oct. 16th, knee-joint suffering from acute synovitis, and a Buck's extension was substituted.

Oct. 18.—Sent to the Colored Home. According to Dr. S. Whitall, in charge at the Colored Home, this man was received and a plaster-of-Paris splint again applied ; and subsequently this was removed and a posterior leather splint applied. There are no farther records of the case.

SINGLE, TRANSVERSE FRACTURE FROM MUSCULAR ACTION—FIBROUS UNION—RUPTURE OF UNION SEVEN WEEKS AFTER FIRST ACCIDENT. —PLASTER-OF-PARIS DRESSING—FIBROUS UNION.

CASE 96.—Wm Edwards, æt.20, residence unknown, slipped and fell May 7, 1869, and was taken to St. Luke's Hospital and limb placed upon an inclined plane. *June* 3, allowed up with limb raised and resting on a chair. *June* 14, crutches. *June* 21, fibrous union—45 days.—Discharged.

Admitted to Bellevue Hospital, June 26, 1869, 3rd Surgical Division.

A few hours before admission to Bellevue he stepped upon a cherry pit on the side walk, and in the attempt to steady himself, felt a pain at seat of fracture.

When admitted, the knee was swollen, hot and painful; the fragments were apparently separated, No crepitus. A straight posterior splint was applied and by his request he was sent to St. Luke's Hospital—Service of Drs. Weir and Hull,—a plaster-of-Paris splint was applied, the fragments being brought together and held until the plaster had hardened.

July 9.—Walking on crutches.

July 17.—Plaster splint removed, and a posterior splint and bandage substituted.

Aug. 13. Discharged, with firm " ligamentous union."

SIMPLE TRANSVERSE FRACTURE—DIRECT VIOLENCE—FIBROUS UNION
—REFRACTURE AFTER TWO YEARS FROM DIRECT VIOLENCE—
ERROR IN DIAGNOSIS—CORRECTED ON 23RD DAY.—RESULT UN-
KNOWN.

CASE 97.—Patrick Gorman, residence unknown, æt. 40, Jan. 17, 1879, fell on right knee. Was admitted to Chambers St. Hospital, and from there sent to Bellevue, 1st Surgical Div. He says that he broke the same patella two years before by direct violence.

On admission there was effusion into joint, general swelling, ecchymosis and pain. Diagnosis not made out. Ice-bags applied.

Jan. 16.—Swelling gone. Diagnosed as a rupture of the tendon of the quadriceps. Tendon drawn up ¾ inch, No crepitus. No evidence of fracture. Adhesive plaster strips were laid obliquely from above around the thigh and carried down over the patella. A horse-shoe strip was laid below the patella, and a buckle supplied. The leg being straight on the thigh and the thigh flexed on the body, a plaster-of-Paris splint was applied, open over the knee. Buckling preferred.

Feb. 10.—To-day recoguized as a transverse fracture of the patella, at its middle. Fragments separated two inches.

March 22.—Splint removed. Fragments separated nearly two inches. Can flex knee about 10°. (No further record.)

SIMPLE TRANSVERSE FRACTURE, FROM MUSCULAR ACTION.—RESULT
UNKNOWN.

CASE 98—John Halton, 385 10th Ave., æt. 32, admitted to Bellevue, 1st Surg. Div., Sept. 25, 1878. On the same day, while in the act of stepping down ten or twelve inches, at the moment when his right foot touched the ground, his knee being a little flexed, he heard a snap and fell.

The fracture was transverse, at the junction of the middle and lower thirds. Slight effusion into joint, but no ecchymosis. Fragments separated 1½ inches. A posterior splint and ice-bags were applied.

Sept. 30.—Adhesive plasters and elastic straps to support the fragments, and a plaster-of-Paris splint, open in front of the knee.

Oct. 1.—Small sheet-lead and wooden blocks above and below fragments, over which the elastic straps were buckled.

Oct. 11.—Apparatus removed. Strips of adhesive plaster of another form substituted to retain fragments; and a plaster-of-Paris splint supported by a posterior wooden splint applied.

Oct. 18.—Left on pass and did not return. (No further record.)

SIMPLE OBLIQUE FRACTURE FROM DIRECT FORCE—RESULT UN-
KNOW.

CASE 99.—Michael Fox, residence unknown, æt. 24, who had suffered amputation of one of his legs five months before and had just left the hospital, fell while walking with his crutches, Dec. 28, 1875, injuring the stump very badly and breaking the patella of the sound leg.

He was admitted to Bellevue, 2d Surg. Div., on the following day. He said he had slipped, and struck the stump upon the flag, and the knee of the other leg, slightly flexed, upon the edge of the curbstone. The stump was badly hurt, but he felt no pain in the knee at the time, and did not suspect a fracture. The knee became greatly swollen and the fracture was not discovered until several days had elapsed. The fracture extended obliquely downwards and inwards, and the fragments were separated 1 inch. The limb was then dressed upon an inclined plane. On the 11th of Jan., 1876, two weeks after the accident the fragments were separated 1½ inches. (Here the record ends.)

SIMPLE TRANSVERSE FRACTURE FROM DIRECT FORCE, COMPLICATED
WITH CONTUSION OF LEG—GANGRENE AND DEATH ON 16TH DAY.

CASE 100.—Allen Block, æt. 45, admitted May 8, 1874, to 2d Surg. Div., having the day before been thrown from a wagon, striking his knee upon the curb-stone. He was taken first to the 99th St. Reception Hospital, where a long side splint was applied, and compresses with "tight bandages" were placed about the knee and splint. When admitted to Bellevue, on the following day, he was found to have a fracture of the left patella, and extensive con-tusion of the leg below the knee. He was a heavy man, weighing over 200 lbs. The limb was permitted to remain in the dressings.

May 9.—Second day ; his general condition was bad. Tympanitis, etc.

May 13.—Sixth day ; a gangrenous slough forming on the leg, below the knee. Applied a posterior wooden splint, the fragments being supported with compresses and adhesive strips.

May 16.—Slough has extended to the lower margin of the patella.

May 21.—Bed sores. Placed upon a water bed.

May 23.—A free incision made to evacuate pus which had formed in the joint. A free bleeding resulted, which was controlled by pres-sure. A consultation was held for the purpose of considering the question of amputation. It was decided that his condition was such that it could not be entertained. On the following day he died.

COMPOUND COMMINUTED FRACTURE FROM DIRECT FORCE—SUPPURA-TION—RESULT UNKNOWN.

CASE 101.—Otto Hoff, æt. 37, laborer, residence unknown. Fell upon a sharp stone, Sept. 16th, 1869, On admission to Bellevue Hos-pital, 3d Surg. Div. same day, the knee was swollen, and there was considerable effusion into the joint. The patella was thought at this time to be broken 'transversely; there was a small wound near its outer margin. Rest and evaporating lotions.

Sept. 27.—Continues red and swollen (erysipelas) Discharging pus from wound. The probe seems to touch the condyle of the femur. Another opening made, which apparently exposes the joint. Poultices.

Sept. 28.—Dr. Smith made a new opening and removed five small fragments, composing about one-third of the patella. The wound packed with picked lint and carbolic acid.

Oct. 2.—Poultices.

Oct. 3.—Opened again.

Oct 4.—Incision over tibia.

Oct. 7.—Incision.

Oct. 8.—Incision; pus fœtid.

Oct. 30.—Condition improved ; poultices suspended.

Nov. 10.—Fifty-fifth day. Posterior pasteboard splint.

Nov. 30.—" Improving slowly." (Here the record ends,.

COMMINUTED (?) FRACTURE FROM DIRECT FORCE. FIBROUS UNION ¾ INCH. (Seen by the writer).

CASE 102.—David King, laborer, æt. 50, 1090 First ave. Admitted to Bellevue, 3d Surg. Div., Jan. 30, 1878. On the same day, while carrying a heavy weight, he slipped and fell on his left knee, causing a " comminuted " fracture of the patella.

On admission, the knee was greatly swollen, and ice-bags were applied.

Feb. 11.—Swelling gone. The adhesive plaster lock-strap was applied, and over this a plaster-of-Paris bandage, enclosing thigh and leg.

March 5.—Splint cut open and renewed ; the fragments being found in good apposition.

April 30.—Splints removed (three months after receipt of injury, and eleven weeks after application of splint). Passive motion employed.

May 4.—(Four months). Discharged cured.

I saw this man Oct. 12th, 1879, nearly twenty-one months after the injury was received. It appears now to have been a transverse fracture through its middle ; there being left no traces of " comminution." The fragments are separated three-quarters of an inch by a firm ligament. No hypertrophy of fragments.

He says that when he left the hospital he was on crutches, and the knee-joint was perfectly stiff. Gradually the motion of the joint returned, but any attempt to flex it forcibly was very painful. For eighteen months he could not put the left foot first in ascending steps, and he has only within a few days been able to return to work. His leg is still unreliable and occasionally painful. He can flex and extend the limb completely.

SIMPLE TRANSVERSE FRACTURE FROM DIRECT BLOW. RESULT UN-
KNOWN.

CASE 103.—Wm. Keating, 861 Third ave., æt. 40. Fell June 11,
1878, while descending a flight of steps, striking upon the edge of a
step. Admitted same day to Bellevue, 2d Surg. Div. There was
general swelling of knee and effusion into joint, and a transverse fracture of the patella. A posterior splint was applied, and the fragments supported with a figure-of-8 bandage.

June 15.—Bandage loose and removed. Fragments separated
half an inch. Crepitus. The limb being elevated and the fragments
pressed together by the fingers, adhesive strips were laid obliquely
from above and below to hold fragments in place ; one strip being
laid over the lower fragment to prevent its tilting ; a roller was applied from the toes to the saphenous opening, and the foot kept elevated.

June 22.—Bandage and adhesive strips removed. Broad strips of
adhesive plaster were then applied, crossing each other above and
below (so I interpret the notes.—H.) to press the fragments together,
and furnished with a buckle. A plaster-of-Paris splint was applied to the whole limb, with a fenestrum over the knee, and the
straps then buckled. (Here the record closes).

SIMPLE TRANSVERSE FRACTURE FROM DIRECT FORCE ; RESULT UN-
KNOWN.

CASE 104.—Mary Moran, æt. 32, 45 West St. Fell out of a window,
Aug. 12, 1877, striking upon her right knee. On the same day she was
admitted to Bellevue, 1st Surg. Div. There was found to be a transverse fracture of the patella below its middle, the fragments being
separated three-quarters of an inch. There was considerable swelling.

A posterior splint, secured at the knee with a figure-of-8 bandage, was applied, and ice-bags.

Aug. 20.—Lock-strap of adhesive plaster substituted for figure-
of-8, and a plaster-of-Paris splint, open at the knee.

Sept. 6.—Removed and re-applied.

Sept. 16.—Much pain in the thigh. Cut open the splint and found that the adhesive plasters had caused excoriations. Plasters removed, sores dressed and a silicate of soda splint applied.

Oct. 1.—Discharged on account of insubordination.

SIMPLE TRANSVERSE FRACTURE FROM DIRECT FORCE—FIBROUS
UNION, ¼ INCH.

CASE 105.—Hugh Dennis, æt. 52, fractured the left patella transversely, at its middle, March 31, 1871. The accident happened in descending a flight of steps with a heavy trunk on his back. Supposing he had reached the bottom of the flight he fell three steps striking upon his left knee, and breaking the patella transversely at its middle.

Admitted same day to 2nd Surg. Div. Fragments separated one inch, but they could be easily brought in contact so as to cause crepitus. Suffering great pain. His limb was at once placed upon an inclined plane, and the fragments secured with circular and oblique turns of a roller.

April 1.—Great swelling. A moist sponge was laid over the knee and bound on with a roller tightly. This being wet at short intervals.

April 11.—Sponge removed. Swelling gone. Fragments separated half-an-inch. A compress was laid over each fragment, and the fragments were drawn together with adhesive plasters laid obliquely. The limb was then enclosed in a plaster-of-Paris dressing. Heel elevated seven inches.

April 14.—Fragments separated half-an-inch. All dressings removed. Broad adhesive strips laid from above and below longitudinally over the patella, and buckled; cork pads being laid underneath, above and below the fragments.

May 9.—Thirty-nine days after the accident, dressings removed. Fibrous union of one quarter-of-an-inch. Upper fragment elevated two lines above the lower at the point of fracture. A posterior splint applied, retained in place by bandages laid obliquely over the knee, etc. (The notes are here terminated.)

SIMPLE TRANSVERSE FRACTURE.—FIBROUS UNION OF ½ INCH. (UNDER
CARE AND OBSERVATION OF THE WRITER.)

CASE 106.—Charles Wormley, æt. 22, fell from a wagon Jan. 26, 1873. On the same day he was admitted to the 99th St. Reception Hospital, and was found to have a transverse fracture of the left patella. Dr. Delgado, my House Surgeon, applied at once a posterior splint, secured with rollers ; that portion covering the knee and the parts just above and below the patella being laid in the form of a figure-of-8.

Jan. 31.—The swelling having subsided, Dr. Delgado applied a plaster-of-Paris dressing.

About the 1st of March the plaster splint was cut open.

March 8.—I found the fragments had united with a ligament of half-an-inch. Fragments could be moved upon each other. Could flex knee about 15°.

SIMPLE TRANSVERSE FRACTURE FROM DIRECT FORCE ; FIBROUS UNION
OF ¼ INCH. (EXAMINED BY THE WRITER.)

CASE 107.—Dennis Sullivan, æt. 25, was struck upon his left knee, Jan. 21, 1873, breaking the patella transversely. On the same day he was admitted to the 99th St. Reception Hospital. The Fragments were separated half-an-inch. The limb was dressed with a long posterior splint ; the foot being elevated.

Jan. 28.—The House Surgeon, Dr. Delgado, applied a plaster-of-Paris dressing.

Feb. 12.—The plaster-of-Paris splint was removed, and adhesive strips and a roller substituted. Two ulcerations had occurred, one above and one below the patella, caused by the plaster ; but these subsequently healed, upon the discontinuance of all dressings.

March 8.—I found the patella united with a ligament of half-an-inch; considerable anchylosis existed. Passive motion ordered.

SIMPLE TRANSVERSE FRACTURE.—FIBROUS UNION OF ¼ INCH.

CASE 108.—James Garlin, engineer, 412 E. 15, æt. 24, fell Sept. 23, 1869, twenty-five feet, breaking the right patella transversely. Does not know how he struck.

Admitted within one hour to Bellevue, 3d Surg. Div. Knee swollen and tense. Lead and opium wash.

Sept. 24.—Ecchymosis on each side of knee. Bursa patellæ distended. Continue treatment.

Oct. 4.—Eleventh day. Not been able to determine the existence of a fracture until to-day, Treatment continued.

Oct. 5.—Thirteenth day. Limb laid upon an inclined plane, the foot being elevated 14 inches.

Oct. 13.—The capsule of the joint is still distended, but the swelling over and about the knee is gone.

Oct. 14.—Three weeks. Adhesive plasters applied to adjust the fragments.

Nov. 30.—Sixty-eighth day. A fibrous union ½ inch in length ound on the fortieth day, but the limb still remains upon the inclined plane, the fragments secured with a figure-of-8-bandage. (The record here closes.)

COMMINUTED FRACTURE FROM DIRECT FORCE, UNION BY LIGAMENT
OF ¼ INCH.

CASE 109.—Daniel Doody, longshoreman, 43 Oliver, æt. 45, broke the left patella by direct violence July 4, 1867. Admitted to First Surgical Division, Bellevue, July 5th. He was suffering also from concussion of the brain, and a fracture of the right tibia and fibula.

There was much swelling about the joint, and an acute synovitis. The limb was therefore placed upon an inclined plane, without being confined in position.

July 27.—Twenty-third day after fracture. The limb was dressed with a leather, posterior splint and bandages.

Aug. 1.—Adhesive plasters employed to adjust the fragments.

Sept. 1.—Fifty-nine days after the accident. All dressings removed. Ligamentous union of one-quarter of an inch in length.

Sept. 17.—Discharged. Laid aside crutches in about three months. Then walked well. Was never in perfect health after this and never worked again. Died March 2d, 1876.

SIMPLE TRANSVERSE FRACTURE FROM DIRECT FORCE—UNION WITH
SEPARATION OF ¼ INCH

CASE 110.—George Galbraith, sailor, 106 Suffolk, æt. 29, fell for
ward striking his knee upon the edge of a step, Dec. 16, 1875. It
hurt him for a short time and he found himself unable to walk.

Dec. 17.—Admitted to Bellevue, 2d Surg. Div. He was found
to have a transverse fracture of the patella, about its middle. The
parts were moderately swollen, but it was not painful. A long posterior splint was applied, secured by a roller.

Dec. 20—Swelling much increased. Lead and opium wash.

Dec. 28.—Twelfth day, swelling gone. "Considerable space between fragments." Adhesive strips were applied longitudinally, and
buckled over the patella, also a roller. On the following day complained that the dressings were painful.

Jan. 6, 1876.—Dressings have been tightened daily.

SIMPLE TRANSVERSE FRACTURE FROM MUSCULAR ACTION—FIBROUS
UNION OF 2 INCHES—NEARLY PERFECT LIMB WHEN SEEN BY THE
WRITER AFTER 5 YEARS.

CASE 111.—Peter Waters, æt. 23, mason, 1830 3d ave , while
running caught his heel, and in his effort to save himself fell back.
At this moment he heard his patella " crack like a fire-cracker," and
found at once that he could not stand.

On the following day, April 30, 1874, he was admitted to Bellevue.
The fracture was found to be transverse below the middle, and
the fragments separated ¾ inch. Evaporating lotions were applied.

May 5.—A silicate-of-lime splint was applied, the fragments having
been previously approximated by adhesive strips locked over the
front of the patella.

May 13.—Splint removed as it did not have sufficient firmness, and
plaster-of-Paris splint substituted, which was soon cut open.

May 13--Seventeenth day.--Discharged at his own request, with instructions to report from time to time. (No farther record.)

I saw and examined this man Oct. 22, 1879, more than five years
after the accident. The fragments were separated two inches, and

united by a firm ligament.   No hypertrophy of fragments.   He can
use the leg almost as well as the other—can flex and extend fully,
and run up and down stairs.

When he left the hospital, with the plaster splint on, he wore it
about two weeks, the joint was then very stiff.   On taking off the
splint he moulded a piece of sole-leather and made for himself a
knee cap, which he wore a few weeks longer.   Subsequently, the
knee being still anchylosed, he consulted a surgeon, who, finding
the upper fragment fixed, pushed it with force from side to side, and,
as he thinks, stretched the ligaments; at least he knows that it caused
him great pain and he could not walk as well as before for six weeks.
Gradually the anchylosis disappeared, and in about one year he resumed work as a mason.

SIMPLE TRANSVERSE FRACTURE FROM DIRECT FORCE—RESULT UN-
KNOWN.

CASE 112.—James W. Hall, cutter, 513 6th ave., æt. 44.   Fell
while running, striking upon his knees, Dec. 24, 1874, breaking the
patella transversely a little below its middle.   Admitted to 1st Surg.
Div. on the same day.

The fragments were found separated 1 inch, and there was considerable inflammation and swelling about the joint.   As a temporary dressing adhesive strips were applied longitudinally and
"locked" over the patella, and there secured by bandages. Lead
and opium wash applied.

Jan. 15, 1875.—22 days after the fracture—A plaster-of-Paris splint
was applied.   (There are no farther notes of this case.

SIMPLE TRANSVERSE FRACTURE FROM MUSCULAR ACTION,—FIBROUS
UNION OF ½ INCH. (Seen by the writer.)

CASE 113.—Samuel C. Milligan, 147 Sullivan St., æt. 39, admitted
to Bellevue, 1st Surg. Div., April 10, 1878.   On the same day, while
carrying a piano down a flight of steps, he put his right foot upon a
step, forcibly straightening his leg, when he felt and heard a snap,
and was unable to stand.

The fracture was in the right patella, transverse and a little below the middle. Ice bags were applied.

April 13.—Lock-strap and plaster-of-Paris splint.

April 25.—Dressings removed, as patient complained of pain. Adhesive extension plasters were arranged above and below the fragments, and the straps from above were carried down the limb and extension upon the upper fragments effected by weights. A dry roller and plaster-of-Paris splint were added.

April 30.—Extension plasters have slipped and caused slight excoriation. Re-applied.

May 13.—Dressings re-applied. Lower fragment has tilted forwards. Adhesive strips laid over it.

May 28.—Allowed to get out of bed, with the extension plasters brought down below the sole of the foot—as a substitute for the weights.

May 31.—Dressings removed and extension plaster strips and plaster-of-Paris splint again applied with a window in front of knee, the extension plaster strips being tightened after the plaster had hardened.

June 8.—Splint removed. Extension upon the upper fragment being made by a piece of elastic tubing attached to adhesive plasters and passed under the foot.

June 25.—Dressings removed.

June 27.—Slight passive motion. Applied a paste-board splint.

July 3.—(About 3 months). Fragments separated about ¼ inch. Knee can be flexed about 25°. Discharged.

I examined Mr. Milligan, Oct. 6, 1879, about 18 months after his discharge from the hospital. He was able to walk without a cane in two months, but wore a knee-cap until about seven months ago. The limb is now as useful as the other. He is a truckman and lifts heavy weights. The fragments are united by a fibrous bond of ½ inch in length, permitting the fragments to move slightly upon each other. The upper fragment is slightly hypertrophied. The motions of flexion and extension are complete and without grating or chafing. He does not drag the leg in ascending steps. I think may be said of Mr. Milligan that his limb is as sound and useful as it ever was.

SIMPLE TRANSVERSE FRACTURE.—FIVE WEEKS BEFORE ADMISSION.
—RESULT PROBABLY FIBROUS UNION OF 1 INCH.

CASE 114.—Anna Benson, 121 William, æt. 28, while walking stumbled and fell breaking the patella transversely through its upper third. She was taken home, and a surgeon called, who encircled the limb above and below the patella, and with counter straps sought to bring the fragments together. This caused much pain. (Whether discontinued or not is not stated.)

Five weeks later, in July 1875, she was brought to Bellevue, 3d Surg. Div. The fragments were separated 1 inch. Adhesive plaster bands were brought from above and below, (underlaid above the patella with several successive layers of adhesive plaster) and "locked," or interlaced, being secured also to a posterior, wooden splint. A plaster-of-Paris bandage, or splint, was then applied.

July 2.—Walking without crutches.

(This concludes the report.)

SIMPLE, NEARLY TRANSVERSE FRACTURE FROM DIRECT FORCE—
RESULT UNKNOWN.

CASE 115.—Michael McDermott, dock builder, 8 Albany street, æt. 32, tripped and fell on his knees, Nov. 1, 1870. He felt a sharp pain in the knee, but with some difficulty arose and walked home. During the next week he sat or hobbled about the house. He kept the knee bandaged.

Nov. 8.—He was admitted to Bellevue, 3d Surg. Div. He was then able to walk, but with difficulty. The patella was found broken nearly transversely, with a slight separation. Extensive ecchymosis, but no swelling. He was ordered to remain in bed.

Nov. 12.—Eleventh day—a plaster-of-Paris bandage was applied to the leg and thigh, the portion covering the knee being laid in the form of a figure-of-8, and over compresses. The limb was then laid upon an inclined plane.

Nov. 14.—He was permitted to use crutches. (No farther report of the case.)

SIMPLE TRANSVERSE FRACTURE—SUPPURATION—"GOOD UNION."

CASE 116.—Mary Dowling, 41 E. 17th st., æt. 55, fell from a second-story window April 7, 1870, breaking the right patella transversely, and also the tibia and fibula of the same leg.

Admitted to 2d Surg. Div., April 8th. There was a wound of about one inch in length over the broken patella, but it did not communicate with the joint. There was considerable fluid in the joint.

The limb was placed in a fracture box, supported by bran bags. On the 9th a plaster-of-Paris splint was applied. On the 13th she was so turbulent and noisy that she was sent to a prison cell. On the 20th, a sinus having formed under the skin, it was laid open. The splint was removed on the 30th of April, and the union found to be "good." It was reapplied and removed finally on the 15th of May. On the 24th she was discharged, the precise result not being stated.

SIMPLE TRANSVERSE FRACTURE FROM DIRECT FORCE—FIBROUS UNION
1·5 INCH.

CASE 117.—Michael O'Neill, laborer, 144 Cherry st., æt. 22, broke the right patella transversely, by falling upon the edge of a stone, March 26, 1869. Admitted on the following day to 2d Surg. Div.

The knee was much swollen and the fragments were separated ¾ inch. Limb was laid upon an inclined plane and cold water dressings applied. As the swelling subsided, by the aid of adhesive strips, the fragments were made to approach each other within ¼ inch.

April 10.—The 15th day—the broken margins were found tilted forwards. Adhesive strips laid across patella. These were removed on the 17th and 21st.

May 6.—41 days—all dressings removed, but patient retained in bed. Fibrous union 1·5 inch.

May 12.—Posterior splint and adhesive plasters.

May 27.—Walking.

June 3.—Discharged.

SIMPLE OBLIQUE FRACTURE FROM DIRECT FORCE—ABSCESS—
"SCARCELY A LINE OF SEPARATION."

CASE 118.—C. Riley, wagoner, æt. 16, was run over by a wagon,
Dec. 24, 1869, and was admitted to the 2d Surg. Div., on same day.

The left patella was broken obliquely, and the joint was considerably swollen. The limb was laid at rest and temporary dressings applied.

Dec. 25.—Only a slight separation of fragments.

Jan. 3, 1870.—Tenth day, pulse rapid, skin hot. Abscess in popliteal region of opposite leg, which was opened. The left leg was then placed upon an inclined plane, and the fragments secured by adhesive strips laid obliquely.

Feby. 7.—45th day, good union. "Scarcely a line of separation."
Discharged.

SIMPLE TRANSVERSE FRACTURE FROM DIRECT FORCE.—TREATMENT
AND RESULT UNKNOWN.

CASE 120.—Jeremiah Sullivan, laborer, 24 Morris St., æt. 32,
slipped with his right foot, falling with his foot under him and striking upon his knee.

Admitted to 3rd Surg. Div. Bellevue, May 4, 1871.

Has a transverse fracture of the right patella.(No farther record).

SIMPLE TRANSVERSE FRACTURE—UNION WITH SEPARATION OF ½
INCH.

CASE 120 —Samuel Hanna, 9th Ave. and 32nd St., æt. 48, admitted to 2nd Surg. Div. Jan. 26, 1873, with a fracture of the patella.
Laid limb upon an inclined plane. In February the fragments
were separated ½ inch.

March .—Plaster-of-Plaster dressing applied.

March 18.—Fifty-one days. The dressings removed. Fragments
separated ½ inch. Knee-joint somewhat stiff. (No farther record.)

SIMPLE FRACTURE FROM DIRECT BLOW—UPPER FRAGMENT "TURNED
UPON ITSELF"—FIBROUS UNION OF ½ INCH.

CASE 121.—Peter Smith, laborer, 714 Water St., æt. 50, was admitted to 1st Surg. Div. Bellevue, Nov. 5, 1867, with a fracture
of the left patella, caused by direct violence. At the time of admission could lift his leg with ease. There was considerable ecchymosis. His limb was placed upon a single inclined plane, and
cold water dressings applied.

Nov. 8.—Longitudinal adhesive strips were applied from above
and below to bring the fragments together.

Nov. 10.—Complains of pain. Adhesive strips removed and re-
applied.

Dec. 26.—Fragments have been kept together as closely as possible with adhesive plaster. Little or no union.

Jan. 9.—Two months after admission dressings removed. No
union, upper fragment "turned upon itself." (There is no farther
record of this case.

Oct, 16, 1879.—Twelve years after the accident, he being then
employed by Mr. Augustus Faber as a gardener. I found the fragments united by a ligament of half-an-inch—the fracture was transverse, below the middle—no hypertrophy. The lower edge of the
upper fragment is quite prominent. He can flex and extend his leg,
but in descending steps he puts the sound limb first. Says he was
four months in the hospital.

SIMPLE TRANSVERSE FRACTURE FROM MUSCULAR ACTION—PROBABLE
FIBROUS UNION—RUPTURE OF BOND OF UNION—PLASTER-OF-PARIS
SPLINT—RESULT UNKNOWN.

CASE 122.—John Herrick, bricklayer, æt. 24. In jumping, Sept.
1, 1878, he felt something give way in his right knee, and on the
following day he was admitted to Bellevue, 1st Surg. Div.

The knee was swollen, ecchymosed and painful, and the fracture
was not recognized. Ice bags were applied and the limb elevated.

Sept. 9.—The swelling having subsided, a transverse fracture of the patella, above its middle, was discovered, the fragments being separated 1 inch." Same splint applied as in the case of Brady." Straps not buckled until the following day.

Sept. 13.—Could not bear the pain caused by the straps and buckles. Adhesive strips applied. In order to relieve his pain and restlessness he was given chloral hydrate and bromide of potassium quite freely.

Sept. 21.—A roller bandage was placed over the patella and beneath the buckles to relieve the pressure of the latter.

Sept. 25.—Dressings removed. Fragments brought together by adhesive strips, and over this a plaster-of-Paris splint the whole length of leg and thigh.

Nov. 6.—Fragments separated from $\frac{1}{4}$ to $\frac{3}{8}$ inch. Can flex knee 30°. Discharged.

Dec. 16.—About three weeks after being discharged he slipped in descending a flight of stairs and ruptured the bond of union. He was re-admitted to Bellevue, same division. The fragments were found separated 1 inch. Suffering no pain. Walking quite well. A plaster-of-Paris splint was applied. It was then cut open longitudinally on either side, and the front portion being open over the knee, the whole was bound on and the upper portion drawn together by straps.

Jan. 17.—Removed and plaster-of-Paris splint applied. Open at knee. Horse-shoe strips of adhesive plaster. (No farther record.)

FRACTURE OF LEFT PATELLA—FIBROUS UNION OF ONE INCH—FRACTURE OF THE RIGHT PATELLA SIX YEARS LATER FROM MUSCULAR ACTION; RESULT NOT STATED—BOTH FRACTURES BELIEVED TO HAVE BEEN SIMPLE AND TRANSVERSE.

CASES 123-4.—Wm. Scott, carman, 122 Amity St., broke his left patella in 1865, when 27 years old, the fracture resulting in a fibrous union of one inch in length. During the four following years he wore a knee brace, after which he walked without any support to the knee, always favoring the injured limb by bearing his weight chiefly upon the opposite limb.

May 16, 1871.—Six years after the first accident, he slipped while walking, and in the effort to recover himself, broke the right patella, and then being unable to stand, settled down easily upon his haunches.

Admitted to 2d Surg. Div., May 18th. The knee was a good deal swollen, and only bandages were applied. The limb being kept at rest.

May 31.—Two weeks after the fracture, strips of adhesive plaster were laid above and below the knee, longitudinally. Plaster-of-Paris bandages were then applied to the leg and thigh, with an interval corresponding to the knee, (not very fully described) and the ends of the adhesive strips were then made fast to the plaster-of-Paris above and below, so as to draw the fragments together.

Sometime in June (date not given) he was discharged, the apparatus having been previously removed; (the result is not stated.)

SIMPLE TRANSVERSE FRACTURE FROM DIRECT FORCE—FIBROUS UNION (PROBABLY)—REFRACTURE FOUR MONTHS AFTER THE FIRST FRACTURE, AND ABOUT ONE MONTH AFTER IT WAS CURED—REUNION.

Patrick Owens, 338 E. 63d St., æt., 28, was admitted to the 3d Surg. Div., Bellevue, Jan. 4, 1877. He stated that he had broken his patella three months before by direct violence, and was taken to the Presbyterian Hospital, and remained there eleven weeks, when he was discharged, with a firm union between the fragments.

One week before admission he fell again, rupturing the bond of union. The fracture was transverse. His limb was placed upon an inclinedplane and the fragments secured by adhesive strips, " locked."

April 12.—About three months after admission he was discharged " cured." (No other record.)

COMMINUTED FRACTURE FROM MUSCULAR ACTION—BOND OF UNION FEELS LIKE BONE.

CASE 126.—Through the courtesy of Dr. E. T. T. Marsh, of this city, I was permitted October 24, 1879, to see John Adkins, 125 W.

30th street, æt 39, who on Jan. 11th, 1877, two years and two months before, while attempting to assume the erect posture with a heavy weight upon his head, slipped, and, in the attempt to save himself, felt the left patella snap.

Dr. Marsh saw him within 30 minutes. The joint was then filled with fluid (probably blood). The fracture was oblique, from within outwards and upwards, and the upper fragment was broken vertically. The main fragments were separated two inches, and the two upper fragments were in contact.

Dr. Marsh applied at once a compress above and below the main fragments, and a figure-of-8 bandage. A few hours later the limb was laid on a single inclined plane—my apparatus—the bandage having been previously removed. Adhesive plasters were applied over the compress and splint, in form of the figure-of-8, and then a roller. The apparatus was continued 28 days, only being renewed once in this time. When removed the fragments seemed to be united. Slight passive motion employed. An open plaster-of-Paris splint was then applied, and this was retained upon the limb until the 48th day, the joint being moved every day. Subsequently a paste-board splint, and finally a knee-cap, which was continued several months. No force was ever employed to overcome the stiffness. He has been at work ever since. Has now very little lameness—indeed none except in descending stairs. The bond of union is so firm that the fragments cannot be moved upon each other. On the outer side they appear to be in contact, but on the inner they are separated half-an-inch. The upper fragments are in contact.

SIMPLE TRANSVERSE FRACTURE FROM MUSCULAR ACTION—UNION FEELS LIKE BONE—$\frac{1}{4}$ INCH SEPARATION. (Seen by writer in 1879.)

CASE 127.—John Rooney, æt. 30, while descending a flight of steps Jan. 7, 1877, " heard a loud snap." At the same moment he felt a severe pain in his left knee and found himself unable to walk. He was at once sent to Bellevue, and admitted to 4th Surg. Div., Dr. Hope, House Surgeon. Fracture transverse at middle ; knee swollen and very painful ; leather splint and ice-bags. The swelling did not begin to decline for some days, and the ice was continued until the 21st. After the 15th the limb was supported by a posterior and leather splint, and the heel raised.

Feb. 2d.—Permitted to leave his bed.

Feb. 17.—"Union firm." Discharged cured.

I examined the leg Oct. 1, 1879. The fragments are united by a firm bond of about ¼ of an inch. It feels like bone. Bends and flexes leg perfectly; walks up and down stairs as well as before ; fragments of natural size ; now lives at No. 73 Fourth avenue, cor. 10th St.; wore his leather splint two weeks after he left hospital ; never wore a knee-cap.

THIRD PAPER.

Total Number of Cases.—127.

Sex.—Males, 99 ; Females, 28.

Age.—Ten years and under, one case. This is the case (52) of the lad five years old in whom, from a direct blow, a small piece of the margin of the patella was broken off.

From ten years, including twenty, six cases ; of which 1 (118) was 16 years old—a boy—the fracture being oblique and caused by a direct blow : 1, (Case 19) was 19 years old—the fracture was transverse and was caused by a direct blow. In this case the ligament subsequently gave way completely on the outside, and a new patella formed in the very much elongated ligament on the inner side. The remaining four cases were at the age of 20 years : all were transverse —two are known to have been caused by muscular action—one by direct force, and in one the cause is not stated.

Until the twentieth year of life then, there were only three fractures, and these were all caused by direct blows. Up to this period, muscular action seems to take little or no part in the production of these fractures.

From twenty years, including thirty, 48 cases. From thirty years, including forty, 33 cases. From forty years, including fifty, 22 cases. From fifty years, including sixty, 8 cases. From sixty years, including seventy, 4 cases. From seventy years, including eighty, 1 case. In this one case, the patient, a woman, was 80 years old.

In all the six cases included in the last two decades—that is from sixty years, including eighty, four are known to have been caused by direct blows, and the remaining case, Bridget Callaghan, 80 years old, fell fifteen feet, and it is fair to presume that the fracture was caused by a direct blow.

It would seem then, that after the sixtieth year, muscular action seldom causes these fractures. The largest number of cases having occurred between the twentieth and fortieth years of life. The total in these periods being 103, out of 122 whose ages are known ; or, if we include the three at the twentieth year, 106 out of 122 cases.

Right or Left Limb.—Of 134 in which this fact is recorded, ninety-three were in the left limb, and forty-one in the right.

Character of the Fracture.—Of the whole number, all were simple except eleven ; and of these nine were comminuted, and two were both compound and comminuted. Of the comminuted fractures, cases 61 and 94, were accompanied with fractures of the thigh also—one died of shock on the fourth day, and one after amputation, rendered necessary by gangrene.

Direction of the Fracture.—The fractures were transverse in 106 cases—not including two which were transverse and vertical (comminuted)—Of these 106 cases, twenty-two are recorded as below the middle of the patella ; sixteen at the middle and seven above the middle.

Cause of the Fracture.—Twenty-five are known to have been the result of muscular force alone; and fifty-eight are recorded as having received blows upon, or as having fallen upon the patellæ, and have been placed in the list of those caused by direct blows. In forty-three cases nothing is said as to the cause.

Of the transverse fractures it will be noticed that a majority of those occurring below the middle are ascribed to muscular action,—that is twelve out of twenty in which the cause is given. Of four oblique fractures, three are known to have been from direct force ; and all of the comminuted fractures except case 127, were from direct blows, as were also the two compound fractures.

Active Synovitis and Bursitis.—I infer that active synovitis ensued in at least thirty-four cases, and probably in many others. Inflammation of the bursa of the patella is mentioned once. Probably in most cases the bursa is torn open as the patella ascends, and communicates freely with the joint, so that bursitis could not be recognized as a distinct phenomenon.

Blood in the Joint, etc.—In case 90, a compound fracture, the presence of blood in the joint was actually demonstrated. Probably it was present in many other cases, but the fact could not be proven. Pretty extensive subcutaneous *ecchymosis* on the sides of the knee and in the ham were very frequently observed.

Treatment.—It will be impossible to summarize the treatment. Nearly all of the recognized plans of treatment were adopted, but in a majority of cases the same plan of treatment was not continued from the beginning to the close ; and it would be difficult in most cases to say to which particular method the result must be ascribed. Of the specific forms of apparatus, there are mentioned, Lousdale's, Wyeth's, Turner's, Mott's, Malgaigne's hooks, Sir Astley Cooper's, both of my own methods, plaster-of-Paris, and other forms of immovable dressings, the "lock strap," "wooden fingers," pully and weights, crescentic pads, and figure-of-8 bandages, also elastic bands, rollers, etc. Most of the patients have been kept in the recumbent posture, with the foot elevated, but some have been allowed to walk about on crutches, especially when either of the forms of immovable apparatus have been employed.

Results.—We now approach one of the most important parts of our subject, and, fortunately, the records are sufficiently accurate and full here to enable us to make valuable conclusions.

It is stated distinctly in 84 cases that the union is fibrous. The bond of union does not permit the fragments to be moved upon each other, and therefore may be constituted of bone, in case 11, and I believe in three or four other cases.

In cases 22, 23 and 64 no union ever occurred. The length of the bond of union is given as $\frac{1}{4}$ of an inch in 16 cases ; $\frac{1}{2}$ in 33 cases; $\frac{3}{4}$ in 13 cases; 1 inch in 3 cases ; $1\frac{1}{2}$ in 2 cases; 2 in 3 cases ; $3\frac{1}{2}$ in 1 case; 4 in 1 case, and 5 in 1 case. The four last cases, or those in which the separation exceeds $1\frac{1}{2}$ inches, are respectively cases 22, 23, 54, and 111. The above records, it will be understood do not include cases of rupture subsequent to union, but only the results of the first treatment. We shall refer to the results after refracture or rupture of the bond of union hereafter.

It is not to be supposed that these estimates of the length of the bond of union are absolutely accurate. Probably the length of the ligament was generally a little longer than is stated, but the records are sufficiently accurate for our purposes. All but 8 are united with a ligament of one inch or less in length, and the largest number have a ligament of only half an inch.

Anchylosis.—More or less complete has existed in nearly all of the cases when the limb was first removed from the apparatus; being most complete, as a rule, in those cases in which the joint has been kept the longest in the dressings, without the use of passive motion.

In no case has force been resorted to to overcome this anchylosis; but it has gradually disappeared under passive and active use of the limb within a year or two.

Rupture of the New Ligament.—The new ligament has given way more or less completely in 27 cases. Possibly we may have included in this number one or two which were never held well in position, such as cases 9 and 32, in which the inner portion of the ligament alone is elongated. This unilateral elongation occurred three times on the inner side and once on the outer. Of the entire number, 5 were gradual, the elongation commencing soon after the patients began to walk; and 18 occurred within ten weeks after the receipt of the original injury, generally on the seventh or eighth week, when the patient in his first attempt to walk has slipped, and the limb has been suddenly bent. After the eighth week there are 4 cases at 3 months, 3 at 5 months, and 1 at 2 years and 4 months (case 18). Case 21 is put down as refractured after 4 years; but the history of the case is doubtful.

I think in the light of this experience it may be said that after the fifth month there is no more danger to the injured limb than to the sound one.

Other Displacements of Fragments.—The lower fragment was found slightly tilted forwards in case 31; and the lower fragment overlapped the upper a little in case 9. The upper fragment was tilted over by the elongation of the inner portion of the ligament in 3 cases, and in the opposite direction by the giving away of the outer portion in 1 case. In case 19 a new patella was formed in the much elongated ligament.

Repetition of the Fracture in the Opposite Leg.—Cases 6, 45, 68, 85, and 124 belong to this class. Perhaps also 59; or it may have been a case of refracture. These latter accidents have evidently resulted from the fact that the sound limb has been compelled to receive alone the resistance in efforts to prevent a fall.

Hypertrophy in Fragments.—This has been especially noticed in 9 cases; namely, twice in the upper fragment alone, once in the lower and six times in both. It is probable that its occurrence is much more frequent than this record implies.

Period of time which elapsed before the functions of the limb were sufficiently restored to resume labor.—Of the primary accidents, that is, of those in which there was no subsequent rupture of the union, I have been permitted to examine 23 cases, at periods of time ranging from four months to twenty-nine years. Only four of these are said to have acquired perfect, or nearly perfect, use of the limb in a less period than two years, although in general they have resumed work within about one year. The cause of this inability to labor has almost invariably been the lack of the necessary freedom of motion in the knee-joint—a partial anchylosis.

It is remarkable, however, that in case 23, a British soldier, there being no union and a separation of the fragments to the extent of 5 inches, he was able to walk well at the end of 29 years, when I saw him. Case 22 was seen after four years with a separation of four inches, and case 54 was seen after seven years, and both walked badly.

Results in cases of re-fracture or rupture of the bond of union—27 cases.—Of 15 cases in which the ligament gave way within a period of three months from the time of the original accident, that is, soon after the union had been effected, 12 have terminated very satisfactorily.   Under a renewal of the treatment the fragments have united with a short ligament.   Case 56, refractured twice, and cases 40 and 47 were not so fortunate.

I do not think that in any case where the refracture occurred later than this was a permanent reunion effected.

FOURTH PAPER.

BEING THE SUBSTANCE OF TWO LECTURES ON FRACTURE
OF THE PATELLA DELIVERED AT BELLEVUE HOSPITAL,
NOVEMBER, 1879.

GENTLEMEN.—The result of my study and analysis of the 127 cases of fracture of the patella, which I have just published in full in the *Hospital Gazette*, are in most points a confirmation of opinions which I previously held, but in some points the conclusions to be drawn are new and surprising; and in either case they merit our careful attention. First, however, I wish to call your attention to a number of cases which I have brought before you to illustrate the usual character and results of these accidents. (Here Dr. Hamilton presented and described about fourteen cases of old fractures of the patella, all of which were united by ligament.)

ETIOLOGY.

First as to the etiology of these fractures. Twenty-five are known to have been the result of muscular force alone; the fractures having occurred without a fall or while the patient was standing, and in some cases when the knee was not bent, the fracture being announced by a distinctly ·felt snap. I believe, however, that muscular action was more or less efficient in causing the fracture, in all of the simple transverse fractures, and in at least one of the comminuted fractures; that is to say in 107 of the 127 cases.

My reasons for this opinion are:—the great power of those four strong muscles which unite to form the tendon of the quadriceps—the fact that ninety-nine occurred in males—that only three occurred in persons under twenty years of age, and only five after the sixtieth year—the largest number being between the twentieth and thirtieth years of life—the remarkable uniformity in the direction of the fracture; and finally because I am unable to cause a transverse fracture on the cadaver by a direct blow.   I might have added also the fact, as attested by museum specimens, that the fracture is very uniformly from before backwards and downwards, as would be the case if it were caused by a cross strain, the active force being attached to the upper fragment.   That the bone breaks most often in the lower third, may perhaps be explained by some mechanical law, but I am not prepared to explain it.

A patella having given way transversely to muscular action, those fibres of the quadriceps which are inserted into the sides of the patella still continuing to act, may break the bone vertically, or cause them to separate laterally.   No doubt this is what happened in case 127.

The source of error in estimating the value of muscular action in the production of this fracture has been, that in the majority of cases the patients have actually fallen upon their knees, and all such cases have been set down as caused by direct force; but in a fall on the knee upon a plane surface, when the leg is flexed to a right angle with the body, the patella does not touch the plane; it is only the tuberosity of the tibia which touches, and the contact with the plane has had nothing to do with the fracture, except as causing, by the concussion, a more active contraction of the muscles already rendered tense by the position and by the effort to prevent the fall.   If a man falls headlong, with his knee slightly bent, the patella may strike the floor, and in this way, and by other methods, the patella may receive a direct blow; but even then, if the fracture is transverse, it is probable that the blow induced the fracture by causing a sudden spasmodic action of the muscles, for as I have said before, we cannot imitate the fracture by a direct blow on the patella of the cadaver.

ANATOMY, PATHOLOGY AND SEMEIOLOGY.

I have already stated that the fracture is almost uniformly transverse, occasionally oblique, and in a few cases the line of fracture is slightly curved; very seldom is the line of fracture vertical.   The fracture occurs most often in the lower third, and least often in the

upper third.   In the transverse fractures the direction of the fracture
is from before back and down.

In a large majority of cases the lesion is limited to the bone, its
periosteal coverings, including the synovial membrane, and the thin
and scattered fibres of the tendon of the quadriceps, which traverse
the front of the bone to become continuous with the ligamentum patellæ.   Perhaps a few of the fibres of the aponeurosis on either side
of the patella give way also, but the lesion of this aponeurosis is ordi-
narily not extensive. For this reason the upper fragment seldom sep-
arates from the lower more than one inch, and in most cases only
about half an inch.   It is only when great and extraordinary muscular
force has caused the fracture that the aponeurosis is sufficiently torn
to permit the upper fragment to ascend two inches or more, and we
may always estimate the extent of this latter lesion by the extent to
which the upper fragment is drawn up.   This is sufficiently illustrated in this dissection, which my Senior Assistant House Surgeon,
Dr. Girdner; has kindly prepared for me.   He has exposed the patella and the quadriceps with its broad lateral aponeurosis, which passes
down, spreading out, to be inserted finally into the sides of the tibia
and fibula at their upper extremities.   He has then divided the patella
transversely with a chisel, leaving the aponeurosis untouched, and we
see now that by no amount of pressure upwards short of that which
causes a laceration of the aponeurosis, can the upper fragment be
made to ascend more than half or three-quarters of an inch.   By cutting the aponeurosis on either side, the fragment can be pushed up
further, but the cutting has to be very extensive before it can be
pushed up three inches, as we have seen has happened in some of the
cases presented to you.   Such extensive separation, therefore, implies
necessarily, extensive laceration of the aponeurosis.

There is another anatomical lesion, the existence of which it may
be proper to assume in the majority of cases, although we have not
the means of demonstrating its occurrence. The posterior wall of the
bursa in front of the knee is probably lacerated, and the joint sur-
faces, or articular synovial capsule is made to communicate freely

with the cavity of the bursa. This bursa is usually present in adult life, and is especially well developed in males. Its posterior wall is composed of a thin synovial membrane, which is in direct contact with the front of the patella and its immediate investments; so that a separation of the fragments to the extent of half an inch could scarcely occur without laying open the bursa. The exception must be found in those cases in which the bursa is not at all or is only imperfectly developed, or the fracture has taken place at a point which does not exactly correspond to the under surface of the bursa.

I have once or twice observed, a few days after the fracture, a fulness in front of the patella so defined as to seem to indicate that the bursa had not been torn, but that it had inflamed and become filled with serum; but I imagine that this appearance might be presented sometimes when a communication with the joint had been established, and the bursa had become filled, its anterior wall being simply pressed forwards by the fluids of the joint.

There remains then, usually, in front of the joint nothing but the skin and a thin layer of areolar tissue, or probably the skin alone, which if it were not at this point very redundant and elastic would often be torn, rendering the fracture compound. In no case has the skin been torn under my notice as an original accident, however much the fragments may have separated, but in one case, not recorded in the preceding report, but which was at the time under the care of Dr. Erskine Mason, the skin was torn in a subsequent accident—a rupture of the new ligament—the fragments being separated very widely. Suppuration of the joint ensued, and it became necessary to amputate at the knee joint by Cardan's method. After which the patient made a good recovery.

It has been found possible sometimes for the patient, immediately after the accident, to continue standing, or even to walk by exercising great care, but in most cases the patients have at once fallen to the ground and were unable to rise.

Very speedily, often within a few minutes after the injury is received, the joint appears swollen. This early swelling must be in part

attributed to the effusion of blood into the joint from the broken patella and adjacent tissues.   The presence of blood in the joint was
demonstrated in case 90, and there can be no reason to doubt that
it is often, perhaps always, present in the joint in some amount, after
the fracture, where it probably undergoes a pretty rapid disintegra-
tion and is mostly absorbed.

There is quite often, also, at an early date, considerable discolora-
tion of the skin on the sides and back of the knee, caused by the in-
filtration of the blood into the subcutaneous areolar tissues.

A synovitis and bursitis (when the bursa is torn) are inevitable
also; the amount of inflammation being more or less in different cases,
but being, in most cases sufficient to. fill the joint with serum and
probably some lymph, within the space of a few hours, or days at most.
This effusion, caused by the synovial inflammation, generally begins
to disappear within a week or ten days, and cannot usually be de-
tected after the second week; but meanwhile, pretty often, a more or
less extensive cellulitis ensues, involving the front and sides of the
knee and extending some distance up and down the limb. Usually this
is moderate, but it has occasionally, and especially when injudicious
pressure has been employed, resulted in suppuration of the areolar
tissue.

PROGNOSIS.

The great number of cases in which the bond of union having been
completed, it subsequently gave way, renders it necessary to speak of
the prognosis relating to a primary accident, and the prognosis relating to a secondary accident, separately.

1. Prognosis in Primary Accidents.—The *bond of union*
is known to have been fibrous in 84 cases, and in no case is it
known to have been bony: but quite often it has been thought
when the patient was first dismissed that the union was bony,
and in each case a much later examination has shown that it was
fibrous. When the dressings are first removed there is often such a
degree of hardness of the tissues between the fragments as to lead
one to suppose that the fragments have united by bone, and they are

so fixed that they cannot be made to move separately, but which deceptive appearance is removed in the course of a few weeks or months. I do not know positively that in any case the union was by bone. If I were to state my convictions I would say, that probably none of the transverse fractures were united by bone; and that only a small proportion of the vertical and comminuted fractures were thus united. Observe I do not deny the possibility of union by bone. A few apparently authentic cases, verified by the autopsy, have been reported from time to time, but I have never seen such a case.

The length of the bond, in primary cases, is usually about half an inch, and ranges from one quarter of an inch to five inches : but of the whole number, there are only five in which the new ligament is more than one and a half inches in length. These are therefore exceptional cases ; and were rendered so by the greater violence inflicted, and the more extensive rupture of the aponeurosis and muscle.

In those cases in which the separation is moderate the ligament will be short ; probably always no greater than the original separation, and in most cases proper treatment will render it less : but in those cases in which the separation is great at first, some have united with very little more than the average shortening, but some remain widely separated, with or without any bond of union.

The fragments have been found *tilted*, in consequence of a yielding of the new ligament, or because of the pressure of the bandages, in four cases. In three of these it was the inner portion of the ligament which had given way, and in one the outer. If from so few examples it is proper to infer the existence of a rule, and to declare that the inner portion gives way most often, we may perhaps find a reason for the rule in the fact that the inner portion of the quadriceps is more powerful than the outer portion, and might therefore act more energetically upon the inner margin of the upper fragment, and cause it to separate more widely from the lower.

Malgaigne made the same observation which I have made, and does not hesitate to make of it a rule, or absolute law; declaring that it is always the inner portion which is found elongated : but I have mentioned one example in which the fact was otherwise. Boyer also alludes to the tendency in the upper fragment to tilt outwards : and both of these writers think that the phenomenon is due to the manner in which the pressure of the apparel was made to bear upon the upper end of the upper fragment. The upper margin of this fragment is not horizontal, but oblique, its outer portion being considerably above the plane of its inner portion; so that any form of adjustment in which the plane of pressure from above, is horizontal, will press more effectively upon the outer than upon the inner portion and cause the upper fragment to tilt, or incline outwards. It seems to me that both unequal muscular action and the direct but unequal, or maladjusted mechanical pressure of nearly all forms of apparel employed to bring down the upper fragment, may be considered as alike responsible for this result. This, as will hereafter be seen, I have sought to avoid by employing a somewhat elastic cotton roller for the purpose of making the downward pressure.

Occasionally it is found, when the fragments have united, that one or both of the fragments are *inclined a little forwards* at the point of fracture, forming an angle salient in front. Usually it is but one of the fragments that is thus inclined ; and in most cases, if not in all, that fragment which is the longest is the one which projects. Thus in cases 9 and 31 the fractures were transverse and in the upper third, and when union was completed the upper margins of the lower fragments overhung the lower margins of the upper.

The longest fragment resting upon a convex surface, and being no longer held in position by a counter force, the ligamentum patellæ or the quadriceps, must inevitably incline forwards. Indeed I have seen this condition present in a recent fracture before any apparatus had been applied; but in such cases very slight pressure, applied from before backwards, was sufficient to restore it to place; and it is quite certain that for this result after union is consummated, the apparatus employed to bring the fragments together is mainly responsible. Both the quardriceps and the ligamentum patellæ have their insertions nearer the anterior than the posterior margins of the patella, a thin layer of tendinous fasciculi actually traversing its anterior face. The upper and lower margins of the patella, therefore, present no elevations for the application of concentric pressure; and if by any form of apparatus, except Malgaigne's hooks, concentric pressure is made, it must be accomplished by causing a depression in these firm ligamentous bands, or a recession from the tegumentary surface, in order that the concentric forces may have a *point d'appui*. This pressure must depress the corresponding margins of the two patellar fragments and elevate their broken margins; and in this case the longest fragment will suffer the greatest displacement. To a certain degree this must occur even with Malgaigne's hooks, as we shall easily see when we consider their mode of application as recommended by himself; but in a much less degree than by any of the other modes of treatment : such, for example, as those in which two hard crescents or a padded ring are employed to bring the fragments together. No doubt it is occasioned also sometimes by the pads which some surgeons place in front of the patella and which get displaced and press unequally.

Both these displacements, namely, the tilting and the forward projection, are imperfections which contribute their proportion to the subsequent maiming; causing in the one case a relative loss of strength in the ligament, and in both cases causing some irregularity in the movements of the patella over the surface of the femur.

There is another form of displacement to which I have not yet referred, but which seems in most cases to be temporary, although it is probable that it is not in all cases, namely, a simple *lateral displacement*. This existed in case 9 before the treatment was fully terminated. The upper fragment was found displaced inwards one quarter of an inch, and it could not be moved from this position—at least not without greater force than it seemed proper to apply. In this case, however, the fragment, subsequently, when he had used the limb some time, gradually loosened and resumed its natural position. I think the same happened in one or two other cases, and that they subsequently came into line. Probably in each case it was caused by the lateral pressure of the bandage or of other parts of the dressing, and might, therefore, have been avoided.

It is easy to imagine that if the fragments are thus displaced the bond of union may be imperfect or unequal on the two sides, or that it might diminish the chances of union, and in either case the evil results might be permanent and serious.

Hypertrophy of the fragments. This must be distinguished from an exostosis, such as is frequently observed along the margins of the fracture, and which is never considerable, only causing a slight irregularity in the surface of the bone, but which may be present without peripheral enlargement or expansion of the fragments.

This actual hypertrophy has been observed by me in nine cases, namely, twice in the upper fragment alone, once in the lower fragment alone, and six times in both. The occasional hypertrophy of the fragments has been noticed by other writers, and Malgaigne has furnished two illustrations of it. The same thing is known to happen pretty often in some of the long bones when broken near their extremities, where the structure is cancellated. I have noticed it often in the fracture of the humerus near its lower end, the lower fragments being in all such cases the ones which become hypertrophied. In the case of the humerus the hypertrophied fragment, sometimes after many months or years, is found to diminish, but whether such a gradual diminution in size takes place in examples of hypertrophied patellæ I am not certain. It has not seemed to me that it does occur.

Period required for recovery of the perfect use of the limb. This matter was referred to briefly in the beginning of my published report of cases. I will quote again more fully what Malgaigne says upon this subject : "Camper has stated that in one or two years the power is recovered, whatever may have been the interval between the fragments. An evident exaggeration, since he himself speaks of a lady with a separation amounting to three fingers breadth, who still limped four years after the receipt of the injury. Mr. Benjamin Bell makes one inch the limit of separation, allowing for the restoration of the firmness of the knee; Boyer follows him; M. Velpeau, on the contrary, affirms that he has seen the functions of that joint completely re-established, with an interval of two or three inches between the fragments. Such assertions are, in my opinion, only accounted for by some inaccuracy of examination, and for my own part I have never seen the functions of the limb completely restored, even when the separation was limited to one third of an inch." *

The fact seems to be that more or less loss of freedom in the motions of the joint and of strength and stability in the limb, remains in the majority of cases for a long period of time, and often during life; but that in a few exceptional cases, where the separation does not exceed one inch, the functions of the limb are completely restored within one or two years. It is remarkable also how well the functions are restored, after a long time, in some cases when the separation is very great, as, for example, in case 23.

The first and main impediment to the restoration of the functions of the joint is the *anchylosis*, which is in many cases at first nearly complete. This anchylosis being due to the passive contraction of the articular ligaments, as a consequence of long disuse, to adhesions and inflammatory infiltrations among the torn muscular and tendinous fibres, and between these latter and the upper fragment of the patella as it lies more or less buried in the torn tendinous tissues. It is never safe to attempt to overcome this anchylosis by force, consequently the process of restoration must be slow and uncertain, and it will generally be found to be many years before the leg can be flexed upon the thigh to the same angle as in the case of the opposite limb.

In a certain degree also the changed relations of the fragments to the articular surface of the femur may be responsible for the lameness.

As to what influence the nature and length of the new bond of union has upon the usefulness of the limb, I am prepared to say, first,

---

* Malgaigne, p. 606.

that the fact that it is generally fibrous and not bony is probably of no consequence, provided the bond of union does not exceed one inch in length. It certainly is in no way responsible for the anchylosis; and, as to its effect upon the stability or strength of the limb, there is no reason to suppose that this slight diminution in the range of the contraction and elongation of the quadriceps will have, after one or two years of use, any appreciable effect upon the stability of the limb. Indeed, so far as I have been able to ascertain, in all of these cases the patients have been able, after a time, to extend the limbs as completely and as forcibly as before.

If, however, the length of the fibrous bond is much more than one inch there is generally an appreciable loss of the power of complete and fixed extension.

We have had recorded too few well attested examples of bony union to enable us to declare whether the fibrous union or the bony union is most liable to a secondary accident—a re-fracture. It would seem reasonable to suppose that the newly formed bone would be thinner than the original bone and less spongy, and that in consequence of its compactness and thinness it would break more easily under a cross strain than would an equally thick, but flexible, ligament. It is well known that a rupture of the ligamentum patellæ or of the united tendon of the quadriceps occurs much less often than a fracture of the patella.

My conviction, therefore, is that a fibrous union of less than one inch in length is quite as advantageous as a bony union, but I do not state this as an established fact.

Refracture.—In the prognosis of original fractures we have to include the danger of a refracture. Indeed, my statistics show a startling frequency of this accident. It is known to have occurred in 25 cases, and in two additional cases the ligament has given way partially. Some of these cases were persons who sought my advice, and they might not therefore correctly represent the true proportion in a given number of consecutive cases, and not one of them were cases which had throughout been under my own care; but, on the other hand, it will be remembered that a considerable number of the 127 cases were not seen or heard from by me, after the treatment was terminated; so that, on the whole, I think that 27 out of every 127 represents the average ratio of these accidents.

A knowledge of this fact, which now for the first time has been revealed to me, is of the greatest importance, as indicating the necessity for great care in the use of the limb after the surgeon has practically dismissed the patient; but it is reassuring to know that two-thirds of the whole number were ruptured very soon after leaving off the apparatus; that is, within ten weeks after the original fracture had taken place; and that five of these took place gradually, commencing when the patient began to walk. Only two occurred later than five months after the injury, or about three months after the apparatus was removed. It would seem, therefore, that it is only necessary to provide against the accident during the first three months after removal of the splint, and that after this a rupture is no more likely to take place than if it had not been broken.

Fracture of the Opposite Patella.—This has happened five times, and was no doubt due in each case to the greater effort made by the quadriceps of the sound limb to sustain the body, when the equilibrium of the body has been disturbed.

II.—Prognosis in Cases of Rupture or Re-fracture.—

A majority of these cases refuse to unite again, whatever means may be employed; and the few cases of success which have come to my knowledge are confined almost entirely to those examples in which the rupture took place very soon after the apparatus was removed, and in which the limb was immediately subjected to treatment.

When the fragments do not unite the patients are for a long time seriously maimed, the limb lacking stability, and often giving way suddenly under the weight of the body. In most of these cases, however, a judicious treatment, such as I shall hereafter indicate, will eventually give considerable stability to the limb, and enable the patient to walk with much safety and ease.

TREATMENT.

Our investigations have brought us to conclude that in a large majority of cases, under any plan of treatment, a fibrous union of the
fragments is all that can be expected; and that probably a fibrous
union, with only a separation of a half or three-quarters of an inch,
is as useful as a bony union.

The only methods which could encourage a reasonable hope of
procuring a bony union, are Malgaigne's hooks, and wiring the fragments together.

Malgaigne's hooks have hitherto not been proven to have accomplished this result, not even in the hands of its distinguished inventor.   In fact, contrary to what I would have expected, there has been
among the cases reported as many examples of fully recognized
fibrous union, as have occurred where some other plans of treatment
have been followed; the fibrous band has been no shorter, and the
number of cases in which a bony union has been supposed to exist
soon after the removal of the apparatus, is no greater than my own
dressings and experience have supplied.

On the other hand, several cases have been reported of dangerous
or disastrous inflammation induced by the hooks, and to this objec-
tion many other methods are never liable.   There seems no possible
reason, therefore, why in any ordinary, simple transverse fracture, in
which the original separation does not exceed one inch or even one
and a half inches, this method should be employed; but in cases in
which the original separation exceeds this, and especially in cases of
a refracture or rupture of the fibrous bond, accompanied with great
separation, it is my opinion that Malgaigne's hooks are entitled to a
farther trial.

As to the method lately suggested and practiced by Dr. Hector
Cameron, of Glasgow, of opening the joint and wiring the fragments
together under carbolic acid spray, and which has been repeated by
Mr. Rose, of London,* and one or two others, I feel in duty bound

---

* Rose, Am. Jour. Med. Sci., January, 1880, p. 278, from Lancet, Nov. 22, 1879.

to say, that it is offering a very grave and dangerous substitute for other perfectly safe, and so far as is yet proven, equally efficient methods; it is hazarding the life of the patient without offering any equivalent. Of the two cases reported by Mr. Rose—one of which he pronounced a bony union, but presented no satisfactory evidence that it was such—Mr. Bryant, who was present, said: "The result in this man's case was very good; that in the woman's case was not so good as he had often seen on the ordinary plan."

Cutting the quadriceps, a method said to have been adopted by Mr. Gould,* demands a very extensive subcutaneous incision, as any one will easily convince himself by looking at this muscle, with its broad and deep tendinous insertion into the top and sides of the patella; and I venture to say that no surgeon has divided all of its fibres, or even the fibres of the rectus, in his subcutaneous incision, and certainly not without carrying his incision freely into the upper part of the joint.

The method employed by Ollier, Goujon and Wyeth (case 47), of injecting between the fragments fresh marrow cells, has as yet yielded no results. Nor do I think it is likely to succeed for many reasons. It certainly, however, has this advantage over either of the preceding methods, that it is harmless.

In order to the accomplishment of the best results, with the least danger to the life or limb, that is, to produce the shortest possible ligament, and possibly to bring about bony union, while the complete integrity of the joint is preserved, there are presented two simple indications of treatment, namely:

First, relaxation of the quadriceps muscle. This indication is accomplished in a small degree by flexing the thigh upon the body: but the effect of this posture is not so great as some writers have supposed. The quadriceps has but one origin from the pelvic bones, and consequently flexion of the thigh does not very greatly relax its muscular fibres. Yet that it possesses some value in this direction is

---

* Gould; debate on Mr. Rose's Case, op. cit., p. 279.

easily demonstrated by experiment. The quadriceps is chiefly re-laxed by extending the leg upon the thigh, that is, by placing the limb in a straight position and maintaining it in this position.

The second indication is to approximate the fragments by direct pressure. Without this pressure the relaxation of the muscle will not bring the fragments into juxtaposition, or even make them ap-proximate this desirable condition.

In order to make direct pressure, surgeons have devised a great variety of methods. They are so numerous, indeed, that I shall not attempt here to enumerate them. Contenting myself with only say-ing that nearly all of them are liable to serious objections, and that none of them are any more efficient than the less complicated plan, which I have now for a long time adopted, and which I shall pro-ceed at once to describe.

Dr. Hamilton's Method of Treatment. (1)—The limb being placed extended, with the foot elevated about six or eight inches, a long splint is applied to the back of the thigh and leg. This splint may be made of leather, of gum shellac cloth, (not felt) with gum shellac, or of any other material having the necessary qual-ities of firmness, lightness and plasticity, so that it can be properly moulded to the limb. Of late I have preferred the gum shellac cloth as possessing in a greater degree the necessary qualities than either of the others. The splint should be long enough to extend from above the middle of the thigh to two or three inches above the heel. Its width should be sufficient to enclose the posterior semi-diameter of the leg and thigh. It should be placed in hot water, and then moulded to the back of the limb; only that it is rather better not to fit it accurately to the popliteal space, in order that a small amount of cotton batting may be placed between the splint and the skin.

The splint should then be removed; and, if made of shellac cloth, in a few minutes it will be sufficiently hard to retain its form. It is now covered completely with a firm cotton or woolen sac, and the sac stitched

---

(1) See illustration of Dr. Hamilton's Splint, p. 13, Fig. 2.

along the back of the splint. The splint being curved to fit the circumference of the limb; the sac must hang loose across the concave surface of the splint, so that the limb may be allowed to fall back to the splint; but the ends of the sac may be drawn and stitched tightly.

One object of the covering is to furnish a protection to the skin against the splint: but the chief object is to supply a basis to which the bandage, which is to enclose the limb and splint, may be stitched. The splint must be applied while the limb is in the position already described; a small wad of cotton batting having been placed in the ham. A roller, made of unglazed cotton cloth, is then turned around the leg and splint to within about three inches of the knee; and another from the upper end of the splint over the splint and thigh to within three inches of the knee. While an assistant approximates the fragments with his fingers, the surgeon makes two or three turns with a third roller around the limb and splint, close above the knee; after which the roller descends below the knee, and an equal number of circular turns are made close below the lower fragment of the patella; and finally, a succession of oblique and circular turns are made above and below the fragments, which turns are to approach each other in front until the whole of the patella is covered—the last turns being again circular. The dressing now being completed, the rollers are carefully stitched to the cover of the splint through its whole length, on both sides; and the limb is left supported in the elevated position by a suspending apparatus, or by some other mode which will ensure its maintenance in this position.

I have been thus particular in my description because all of my hearers may not have had experience in the application of bandages, and because to many of the details I attach importance. A few words of explanation of some of these points may not be amiss.

The cotton cloth roller is preferred, especially for the purpose of approximating the fragments, because, if unglazed, it yields a little, and adapts itself smoothly to the skin, even sinking down a little just above and below the patella, thus rendering it less liable to slide over the patella. Reversed turns are omitted altogether because they cause sharp cords where they are folded, and sometimes produce painful constrictions and excoriations. Adhesive strips recommended by me in the first edition of my work on fractures, I have long since laid aside. They are just as liable to slide ; they are apt to cut at their free margins, and they have to be raised up from time to time to be tightened, and they cannot be stitched and thus permanently secured to the cover of the splint. No pads above and below the knee are recommended because they are apt to become displaced, and if they remain in place they no more effectually press the fragments together than does the cotton roller. No pad is placed in front of the patella because the last turns of the roller press back the fragments as effectually as a pad. Care must be taken when the roller is applied and the fragments are approximated, that the loose skin in front of the patella is not pressed between the fragments. No lotions must be applied, to saturate the dressings. They render the skin more liable to excoriations and they are in no way useful.

All that remains to be done is easily said. On the second or third day the swelling of the knee will be found, probably, to have subsided some, and the oblique turns of the bandage from above and below the patella, will need to be tightened. This will be done by over-stitching, with strong thread, the oblique turns. Taking care to do this on both sides and so far back that the doubling of the cloth will not be over the sides of the exposed portions of the limb. The same thing may be required to be done every day, or every second or third day for two or four weeks. Meanwhile it will generally be found—for the position of the fragments can always be felt—that the space between them has not been increased, and in most cases that it has sensibly diminished from the day of their first adjustment.

At the end of about four weeks the apparatus should be removed carefully. It is now observed generally, that the knee is pretty stiff, and that the upper fragment cannot without considerable force be displaced in any direction. It is anchylosed, and there is very little danger that it will thereafter draw up farther, and it is not probable that any apparatus will make it descend. But as a matter of safety,

an assistant should now press the upper fragment gently downwards·
while the surgeon flexes the knee very slightly, so as to diminish its
stiffness. He ought, in doing this, never to cause pain or to use any
degree of force.

The splint is then to be reapplied in the same manner as before.
Daily, hereafter, the splint should be removed with the same care and
the limb gently flexed. In the meanwhile the patient may go about
upon crutches if he chooses.

In six or eight weeks the bond of union may be considered completed, and the patient may be dismissed from the immediate care of
the surgeon, but not until he has been fully informed of the danger
of a rupture of the new ligament, and has been provided with the
means of protection as far as possible. He must be taught that for the
next three or four months this danger is great ; and that any sudden
flexion of the limb may cause it ; and indeed that it may be caused
by simple muscular action, when the limb is not flexed. During this
period he should walk only upon crutches, and the knee joint should
be constantly supported, unless he is completely at rest.

The knee-caps usually furnished for this purpose are wholly unreliable. They allow the knee to bend too freely. Indeed, nothing
but an inflexible splint can ensure safety; and the same splint employed in the treatment reduced one-half in length, and secured by
straps and buckles, is the best I have yet employed.

Under no circumstances, in my opinion, is the surgeon justified in
attempting to overcome the anchylosis by force, either with or without an anæsthetic. The chances are more than equal that he would
substitute an ununited patella for an anchylosed knee. In time, and
generally within a year or two, the anchylosis will disappear under
careful and moderate use of the limb.

It will be seen that I no longer recommend the wooden inclined
plane, figured in my " Treatise on Fractures and Dislocations." The
principle of its construction is correct, and the results have been
satisfactory, but it is unnecessarily cumbrous.

Plaster-of-Paris dressings are simply means of keeping the limb straight, and for this purpose they are heavy and present no advantage over the splint I have recommended.   The limb soon shrinks under the splint and they lose in two or three days all control over the fragments.   They conceal the fragments entirely from observation, except when they are now and then removed, and this is done seldom, because it is always a work of some labor.

I now come to consider briefly the treatment of a *refracture* of the patella, or a rupture of the newly formed ligament.

In all cases the patient should, as soon as possible, be subjected to the same plan as I have recommended for original fractures, only that the treatment will have to be continued longer, and with smaller hope of a reunion.   It is here when the separation is great, and in old cases of ununited fracture, that I could justify the use of Malgaigne's hooks: and of their value even in these cases I am not prepared to speak confidently.

The time always arrives, according to my experience, in which supporting and retentive apparatus is worse than useless.   The period is within five months after the original accident, or within about three months after the union of the fragments.

A reference to some of the cases I have reported, and especially to that of Asst. Surg. Myers, of the United States Navy (case 40), will illustrate the importance of removing all support and teaching the muscles to rely upon themselves alone.   Under proper and free use of the limb, aided by friction, electricity, etc., the muscles will become developed in size and strength, and through their remaining attachments to the sides and front of the leg, below the knee, will give to the patient often a very useful limb.

THE END.

www.ingramcontent.com/pod-product-compliance
Lightning Source LLC
Chambersburg PA
CBHW032155010726
47493CB00008BA/2703